What the Birds See

What the Birds See

SONYA HARTNETT

CANDLEWICK PRESS
CAMBRIDGE, MASSACHUSETTS

First published by Penguin Books Australia, 2002

First U.S. edition 2003

Library of Congress Cataloging-in-Publication Data

Hartnett, Sonya.
What the birds see / Sonya Hartnett. — 1st U.S. ed.
p.   cm.
Summary: While the residents of his town concern themselves with the disappearance of·three children, a lonely, rejected nine-year-old boy worries that he may inherit his mother's insanity.
ISBN 0-7636-2092-0
[1. Loneliness — Fiction.   2. Missing children — Fiction.]   I. Title.
PZ7.H2285 Of 2003
[Fic] — dc21   2002073717

2   4   6   8   10   9   7   5   3

Printed in the United States of America

This book was typeset in Caslon.

Candlewick Press
2067 Massachusetts Avenue
Cambridge, Massachusetts 02140

visit us at www.candlewick.com

For Evelyn McAlister,
to remember her mother, Peg

IT WAS A WARM DAY AND THEY HAD BEHAVED, AS THEY had promised they could, so there must be ice cream. Veronica took her sister's hand. That afternoon, so near to winter, the sky was very blue; the sun felt soft as a cat. The children, on the footpath, paused to wave to their mother. For them, at their age, a trip to the shop could take on the dimensions of a voyage.

The mother straightened from the soil, hair falling into her eyes. Her children's voices were thin and high, the piping of chicks in a nest. "Goodbye, my loves," she said, the words no more than her habit. The mother would remember, later, the white glint of silver coins held tight in the palm of her son.

Christopher was five, with a child's ponderous gait; his older sisters, leggy as fillies, must match their pace to his. Zoe's thoughts would drift as she ambled, lingering on insects and flowers. Bending again to her garden, the mother knew without calculation that her children would be gone for half an hour: fifteen minutes to the shop, fifteen minutes home.

The route they'd take to the shop would bend around four corners of the suburban neighborhood: two right turns, two left. Their neighborhood was a modest one, and the distances between the corners were not great. The result of all the twisting was that no one who saw the Metford children walking through that clear afternoon would see them for very long.

The first witness was changing a tire, on his knees uncomfortably on a stone driveway. He noticed the children because the little boy, passing the gate, made an infant's noise for a car, *brrm*. The sound made the man smile, the only thing to have done so all day. The witness recognized the Metfords as local, although he did not know their names. He would tell the police that, when he saw them, the children were alone.

The youngsters had rounded the first corner, a right turn, when they were seen again. This witness, a woman shaking crumbs from her kitchen mat, also recognized them, having walked on countless occasions past the Metfords' picket-fenced front yard, where the children often played. She saw that the eldest girl, ten-year-old Veronica, was holding her brother's hand. The girl's pale hair caught the light, a flag of sunshine down her spine; the boy's blue shadow yearned out from his feet, lean and gangle-limbed. The middle child, Zoe, wandered behind her siblings, lashing a eucalypt switch through the air. Following her was a man, fair, quite tall, thin. He wore his lank hair fashionably long. The witness assumed that this man was with the children, for he walked just a step behind.

Two corners later, the Metfords were seen for a third time. The frenzied barking of a terrier made its owner look up from a crossword. Through a window he saw the children step uneasily onto the nature strip, putting distance between themselves and the unfenced canine. He saw the older girl say something to the small ones, stern and reassuring. The children kept to the grass, Veronica shepherding her brother protectively, until they were beyond sight of the house. The dog did not chase them but gave a final militant bark. It trotted across the nature strip and sniffed the footprints in the weeds. There were other smells that must be investigated too. The owner watched until his pet returned satisfied to the veranda, resuming its vigil. This witness would insist that at no time while he was looking into the street did he see a man of any description trailing the three children.

3

Outside the shop, they were noticed again. This would be the last sighting. A woman, checking her change in the shade of the store, saw from the corner of an eye a little girl waving. The woman was a schoolteacher, and her first instinct was to assume the child was one of her pupils— Zoe Metford, blue-eyed with mousy bobbed hair and a round, elfin chin, looked, at a glance, like any other seven-year-old. Not recognizing her, however, the teacher turned to discover the recipient of the child's friendliness. On the far side of the road, a young man was standing beside a street sign. The witness would describe this man as thin, tall, unhealthy. His brown hair was windswept and clung about his shoulders. He wore blue jeans and a T-shirt, ruby red against his skin. Over a wrist was hanging a colorless cloth of some kind. He did not return the little girl's greeting, and the teacher guessed she had made a mistake. The children and the youth had nothing in common, and perhaps the child was waving at a bird. As she walked away, the teacher smiled to see the difficulty the older girl was having, prizing coins from her brother's clenched hand.

In 1977, a Year of the Snake, the purged Chinese leader Deng Xiaoping was returned to power. The audacious angles of Concorde took to the air, linking Paris to New York. Queen Elizabeth celebrated her Silver Jubilee, *Time* magazine named Anwar Sadat its Man of the Year. Disco ruled the dance floor, jiving to *Saturday Night Fever*. The space shuttle *Enterprise* successfully completed its first manned flight, and *Star Wars* was seen by millions. A fishing boat dredged from the Pacific's depths a carcass initially touted as being that of a dinosaur. The United Nations banned the sale of arms to South Africa, U.S. President Carter officially pardoned those who'd draft-dodged the Vietnam War. The Altair 8800, the first true personal computer, was released for sale in kit form. Soccer star Pelé retired from the game; comedian Groucho Marx took his final curtain call. The credits rolled over actors Joan Crawford and Charlie Chaplin. Elvis left the building, beached ignominiously on his bathroom floor. In the Canary Islands, two 747s collided on a runway: more than 570 people were killed, making this the greatest aircraft disaster in history.

Three children bought no ice cream, did not return home.

One

They have found a sea monster. A Japanese fishing boat, trawling for mackerel in the deep black seas off New Zealand, has caught in its nets the shabby stinking remains of a colossal beast. The crew had hoisted the rotting thing over the boat to get a better view. At first they'd thought it was a whale—then they wondered if it wasn't something more. As if obliging the curious men, the dead thing had slithered through the ropes and slumped heavily onto the deck. Pinching their noses, gagging, the fishermen reeled away. One held his breath to creep gamely forward, camera in hand to record the astonishing wreckage they saw.

Adrian stares at the photographs, reproduced imperfectly in the morning's newspaper. In the background of each picture are the beams and steel cables of a working trawler; in one there is a checkered lifesaver ring. Massed in the foreground of the photos sprawls the monster. Its blockish head weighs down a long and narrow neck. Winglike flippers fold back from its cresting, cavernous body. It seems to possess a tattered rope of tail. The bones show through—sometimes break through—the white and waxy skin. The flesh looks melted; it is a thing in ruins. Seaweed hangs from it in hanks. Knuckles on its backbone are as straight as a set of stairs.

There's speculation that this creature could be a giant turtle, slipped loose from a massive shell. There is even talk that it might be a plesiosaur, which is a seafaring dinosaur believed extinct for millions of years. A spokesman calls it a precious and important discovery; a toy company announces it will sell wind-up models of the thing.

They hadn't kept it on the boat for long. It had stunk unbearably. After the photos were taken, they'd jimmied it off the deck, once more into the sea.

A monster. Adrian scoops his spoon through the limp flakes and warm milk of his breakfast, studying the photographs. There's something sad in the way the animal hangs its head, its attitude of defeat and shame. It is sad that it's been dredged from its cold-water grave and hung up for everyone to see.

Still, a *sea monster*. In the pictures, the men who stand beside the beast look like children, even smaller. Though this one is dead, there might be others alive, winging the scaly waves into shore. It is not going to be the same now, swimming in the sea.

Adrian adds sea monster to the list of things he finds disquieting.

Grandmother (Grandmonster?) is another. After breakfast she makes him stand in front of her dressing-table mirror while she combs his hair. She makes no attempt to be gentle. Adrian, looking in the mirror, winces occasionally. His hands hover just above the surface of the dressing table.

"Don't fidget, Adrian."

"I'm not."

But his fingers are drawn like thieves to the glittering dresser set that holds pride of place on the tabletop, a hand mirror and hairbrush rested on a matching sparkling tray. Apart from the squat mirror face and the prickly bristles of the brush, the entire set is made of crystal. The crystal is carved into a pattern of neat rowed pyramids. Running a finger over the pyramids feels like petting a crocodile. Adrian lifts the hairbrush by the handle, and the weight of it makes the points of the pyramids bite into his palm.

"Put it back now."

He returns the brush carefully to the tray, bristles down, beside the mirror, but his fingers linger, balancing on the pyramid tips. "You never use this brush and mirror, do you, Gran?"

She doesn't look up from the knot she's discovered. "It's too good to use."

"Then why do you have it? Why do you keep it on the table?"

His chin is jerked up as she wrenches the knot, and he hears his hair tearing. "If we only kept what had a use," she says, "there'd be a lot less junk lying round."

He contemplates her image in the dresser mirror, wondering what she means. He's never seen much junk lying anywhere around the stolid urban neighborhood, but he imagines tottering tangles of doll heads, bike tires, and foil milk bottle caps rising as creaky mountains from the middle of footpaths. He scrambles like a mouse to the peak of a rubbish hill, and as far as he can see is inviting flotsam and curious dregs, a child's utopia. He returns his gaze to the silvery mirror: his gran is wearing a cream

dress splashed with flowers so red they might be bleed-
ing. "Crystal looks the same as glass," he muses. "What's
the difference?"

His grandmother doesn't answer. He shifts his balance to the other foot. "I don't know why there's two
things that look the same but get called different names."

"Adrian, stand still!" She cuffs the side of his head, and
he straightens obediently, dropping his hands to his sides.
In the mirror she's frowning furiously at his hair. His hair
is dense and yellow and strangely, stiffly wild, an armload
of hay dumped helter-skelter on his head. It tangles like it
has a lunatic mind of its own. "Where on Earth did he get
this hair?" his gran asks no one, and strand after strand of
it breaks beneath her plowing comb. "It didn't come from
our side of the family. The McPhees haven't got this
impossible straw. It's come from the father's side."

Adrian steals a cowed glance to the mirror. His
grandma's hair sits in downy cylinders—if he opens the
top drawer of the dresser, he'll find the pink and blue plastic rollers responsible for curving it that way. Her hair looks
white as chalk today; it is thin, and getting thinner. He
seems to remember it once being mauve. He dreads the
thought of sprouting purple hair himself, but he worries
that he'll never be a normal person, that his impossible hair

11

is a symptom of some inescapable failing. Even when his grandmother has finished with it, the hanks still seem defiantly snarled. "There," she says. "You're ready."

Adrian's gaze flits to his reflection, his clean face, his trim school uniform, the sky-blue collar at his throat. The V-neck sweater sports cuffs of navy blue; the gray corduroy trousers are ironed. This is *ready*. Though it is the brink of winter, the past few days have been warm, and the corduroy will be heavy to wear. In summer the boys wear shorts and long socks, and their kneecaps look bruised, knobbled, too big for their legs. His gran says, "Get your things and I'll meet you in the car."

He hurries down the hall to retrieve his satchel from his room, a hand on his forehead to soothe the smarting of his scalp. He double-checks the bag's depths for his homework and lunch box. As he trots back through the hall, the strap of the satchel like a swinging snake on his arm, he hears his uncle calling him and slides to a halt on the parquetry, teeth sinking into his lip.

The door is slightly ajar. Adrian runs a hand down it lightly, so it glides away on its hinges. He slips partway through the gap, an arm and foot and the school bag staying in the hall. The room is dark, the curtains closely drawn. On the cold air is the ruddy mean scent of oil paint

12

and, beyond it, another, insistent and grimly stale: this is only the smell of young man, but Adrian sniffs in it the odor of the bad things that can befall anyone. "Yes, Uncle?"

The dark and silence has made him whisper. A scrap of brightness noses in from the hall but is parched before it reaches the end of the bed. Adrian knows his uncle is lying there, curled like a mole under his earthy heap of blankets. His pillow, Adrian knows, is limp and dented as a fallen leaf. Again he breathes, "Yes, Uncle?"

Uncle Rory speaks into the black; his voice is like the snow. He says, "You tell me something and I'll tell you something."

A fishhook of dread grabs at Adrian's maw. He hears, outside, the engine of the car. His grandmother is reversing the vehicle out of the garage. The car is as big as a tank, as an ocean liner, and it takes all his grandma's patience to get it safely down the drive. If he is not there to meet it when the wheels heave onto the footpath, then—strife, grandmonster. The inspiration comes with giddying relief. "They've found a monster in the sea."

"Have they?"

"Yes—in the newspaper. It might be a dinosaur."

"Really." He hears the air jet from Uncle's nose. "We'll see."

13

Adrian can't think what to answer; his ears are pinned back with the sound of the car. The bag dances on the end of its strap. "I've got to go."

"Don't you want to hear what I'll tell you?"

He nods quickly and swallows. His uncle shifts, the blankets distend, and the bed creaks tiredly. "I'll tell you the difference between glass and crystal, Adrian. The difference is that crystal sings."

Adrian blinks. Uncle Rory hears everything—Adrian often forgets. Uncle is a man who hears and sees all: Gran says it's because he won't stir himself to do anything a bit more useful. Rory would have heard Gran disown Adrian's unwieldy hair; Uncle himself has the McPhees' puckish but biddable curls. "Oh," says the boy.

"Do you know what I'm talking about? How crystal sings?"

". . . No. I've got to go."

"Trust me," says Rory. "It sings. One day I'll show you."

Adrian looks blindly into the room, the air chill on his lips. The smell is almost solid; the scrap of light from the hallway has fainted across his shoes. "I've got to go," he repeats.

"Go on, then," sighs his uncle. "Pay attention to your teacher."

"I will," says Adrian; he ducks away and runs down the hall, flying like a bird, through the kitchen, out the door, and into the morning air.

He doesn't like or hate school: his nine years have been lived doing what older people have told him to do, and going to school is one of those things, unavoidable, not worth resenting. This isn't his first school—he's been coming here only as long as he's been living with his grandma and uncle, which is almost a year. Before then, while he'd lived with his mother, he had gone to a school so close to home that he'd walked there and back alone every day; living with his father, he'd caught the school's trundly bus. Now, at this different school, his gran drives him to the gate each morning and meets him in the same spot every afternoon. She often tells him he's a *tie-down*, and Adrian has no clear idea what she means. He doesn't have anything to do with ties.

He isn't particularly gifted at anything except art: the other kids gather admiringly round his desk during the once-weekly afternoon sessions when they're allowed to paint and draw. Aside from this, he goes more or less ignored. He doesn't mind that—he prefers to be overlooked. He is bashful and rarely puts up his hand: if he knows an answer, he generally keeps it to himself. He isn't boisterous; he can't run fast; he is hopelessly uncoordinated. He sometimes joins the boys playing soccer at lunchtime on the broken asphalt, but he isn't a skillful player. When the captains pick their teams from the mob, first one boy choosing and then the other, Adrian is unfailingly one of the last to be selected, left waiting with the fat boy and the immigrant. Adrian is the runt. But he takes the humiliation in good stead and always feels a squeeze of pleasure when his name is finally called.

He has a best friend, another unathletic specimen: Clinton Tull, whose glasses are thick enough to hold back the tide, never sees a soccer ball coming before it booms off his brow. Clinton is known to be scrupulous, and his glasses naturally make him wise. He is regularly called upon to settle disputes that fisticuffs have failed to solve. He isn't spoiled, but his mother delights in buying him things. The two boys had become friends over a top-of-the-range tin of Derwent pencils: Clinton owned them, but Adrian could harness their brilliance.

Most lunchtimes Adrian doesn't play soccer; instead, he and Clinton sit in their favorite place on the sidelines, watching and conferring quietly, somber as a pair of old gents. They sit side by side with their spines against the red bricks of the disused restroom building, their wrists propped on their knees. The bricks are warm in winter, and the eaves shade off the summer sun. Attached to the wall, at ear height to the sitting boys, is a steel trough with six drinking taps, and occasionally they exchange a few words with a bloodied or thirsty soccer player. From their territory against the restrooms, the boys overlook most of the school yard—the basketball court where the bigger girls play softball; the undercroft where the smaller girls skip; the asphalt yard that's a black, gnarled, and grassless playground; the jungle gym and monkey bars over which the little kids swarm. They see the studious girls ranged in twos and threes along a distant fence, driving unsentimental bargains over trading cards. They see the excluded boys and girls, most of them sitting in shadows by themselves. Adrian feels sorry for these misfits, but not so sorry that he will risk his meager reputation by befriending any of them. He knows how close he himself teeters to the abyss of exclusion. Only Clinton stands between him and the searing loneliness Adrian recognizes in the outcasts. He has felt, before, their aching forlornness for himself.

It is a small suburban school, and the pupils know each other's faces and names. There are entire families on

17

the roll call, siblings spread throughout the grades—even Clinton has a sister in prep. Everyone knows who is rich, who is poor, whose mother is expecting another baby, who was sprung on the weekend pitching water bombs at the presbytery door. Between classes the yard swells with normal school sounds, laughter and shrieking, whistles and tears, the warm bubbling welter of childhood's noise. But through this school runs a streak of strangeness, and ever since the day Clinton explained it to him, Adrian has never felt very safe here.

Along the road from the school, enclosed by a towering fence, stand the long russet buildings of St. Jonah's Orphanage. A few of its charges attend the school. The stigma of the institution hangs from them like a fusty, wet-wool smell. Many of the most isolated children, the ones sunk most deeply into the lunchtime shadows, are children from St. Jonah's; other children shy from them. "Because it's not really an orphanage," Clinton had informed him, early on. "It's a Home."

Adrian, confused, said, "I thought they didn't have homes?"

Clinton's face had creased, his glasses dropping to the end of his pebble-round nose. He is a font of innuendo and gossip—his parents approach life as a soap opera and make dramas out of the most mundane, worrying details to death over the dinner table, the steaming peas. "Not a home, a *Home*. Like an orphanage for kids whose mum and dad are still alive."

"How come they're at the Home, then?"

"Their parents are no good, that's why. Can't look after their children. Don't treat them very well. Maybe don't even want them. So the kids get taken away and put in the Home. But it's too late, usually. Some of them have already gone nuts. Nuts from not being looked after properly. Crazy like their mum and dad are."

Adrian had felt the warmth drain from his skin. His own parents were alive, but he didn't live with them. He had prayed that Clinton would not make a contorted connection between himself, his absent parents, the craziness of the Home children, and the possibility that Adrian might likewise be crazed. Clinton had said nothing, either his imagination or his malice failing to stretch so far. But Adrian had thought of it, the similarities seemed glaring to him, and he still thinks of it every day. He is haunted by the prospect of becoming a pariah here, distrusted and pitied and sometimes openly despised, ground down beneath the mercilessness of the fresh-faced young.

The pair of them sit against the restrooms this lunch-time, sunning in the last warmth of autumn. They have already discussed the sea monster; Clinton is laying private plans to catch a living one. He is a boy with ambitions, his mother always telling him that he's destined for glory: he sees himself as a seafarer, the creature bound in iron and chain. Now there's nothing left to talk about, and their gazes drift across the yard, where a desultory but painful game of dodge ball is being played, to the log-lined perimeter of the adventure playground. Prancing there, on her toes, is the girl the children call Horsegirl.

She is the most unlovely and unloved of the Home children, and the most defiantly crazed. Her real name is Sandra, but it is rarely heard: inside the classroom, the teacher directs few questions to her. She is sometimes unruly in class, slamming her fists on the desk, mumbling hotly to herself. She is tall and strong and exudes danger—everyone is frightened of her. When enraged she is near impossible to control, and the male third-grade teacher has often had to be called. She becomes enraged if the authorities don't let her do as she pleases, so she is mostly left to do what she likes. And what pleases Sandra is to be a horse.

She trots, prances, gambols like a horse. She tosses her long mane of hair. She paws the asphalt and shakes away flies. She often won't talk, for horses never do, but she snorts and nickers and neighs, smacking flaky raw lips. Sometimes she confines herself to the make-believe stable that she's outlined with pine needles and cones. If she is in a nice mood, she'll hoist a prep child on her shoulders and race around the yard. Her mood might blacken doing so, and the child becomes her terrified prisoner. Then there's screaming, shouting, teachers white with stress. The result of Horsegirl's volatility is that when the children see her coming, they tend to back away. Nobody wants to be accused of laughing at her, so their faces go carefully blank. No one talks to her or meets her eye, not even the big boys from the higher grades. In the classroom, no pupil will share a desk with her. She is relegated to a lonely corner, where she is happiest.

Today something unusual has happened, and no one can remember seeing Horsegirl so cheery. She has brought to school a leather bridle and reins. Nobody knows where she got these from, and none dares to ask. A nun at St.

Jonah's has doubtlessly indulged her, realizing the girl's mind has galloped beyond repair. If she must be a horse, let her be a joyous and fulfilled horse.

Horsegirl is running round the yard, pausing occasionally to buck. She has the bit in her mouth, the reins slapping at her legs. Above the noise in the yard, Adrian can hear the clink of the bridle's buckles. The air is cut through with sharp, surprising whinnies. She makes a sound when she canters, a fair rendition of hooves striking dirt. Children fall away to give her space to run. Her thin gray face is pink with exertion, her expression bliss: in her mind she is thundering somewhere far from here. Somewhere green and hilly, Adrian thinks, where nothing catches her. Clinton's eyes, behind masses of glass, follow her back and forth.

"Look at that," he says. "That's what happens."

Two

Beattie cooks Adrian's dinner early, while it is still light; he perches at the kitchen table, frowning his way through his homework, while she fries an egg and a pair of skimpy sausages. He has to put his books aside and eat at the table, but he's allowed to take his dessert into the den and eat that in front of the television. He curls in one of the big leather chairs with a bowl of ice cream drenched with chocolate topping from a bottle. His grandmother supposes it is bad for him, having so much syrup that the white globes of ice cream are floating and drowned, but she also thinks that, in this life, there are more important things worth worrying about.

One of them is on the TV.

The news is showing images of the scene of the crime: the shop, the house, places along the route the children traveled between the two. When the reporter mentions ice cream, Beattie sees Adrian lick syrup from his lips. He asks, "Is that close to here?"

"Twenty minutes in the car," says Rory.

"Shush!" snaps Beattie.

The color dial on the television is turned a fraction too high. The shots of the Metford garden are gaudy green, the picket fence clashy white. The dress worn by the mother is a tint of hysterical orange. She is filmed walking toward the garden gate, leaning on the shoulder of a slightly doughy man. He must be the father, holding a hand out before him as if unseen obstacles hamper his way. The woman seems weak, as though the strength has been extracted from her using a method that has also reduced the years she will live. The couple are shown getting into a police car, the man's arm guiding the woman's shoulders, and Beattie clicks her tongue. It's a picture that makes the mother look guilty of some wrong.

After the shot of the police car, photographs of the children are flashed. Veronica has fair hair, the kind of blond that never looks clean. She is cuddling a flop-eared rabbit to her chin. Zoe has freckles across her nose, standing stiffly in her best dress clutching a present wrapped for a friend. The photograph of Christopher shows him reaching for the handle of a lawn mower, his upturned face full of giggles. Christopher, the reporter says, has asthma and needs medicine.

The image of the laughing boy is replaced by the black-and-white sketch of a man seen in the vicinity of the ice-cream shop. His hair hangs lifeless on his head, long around the shoulders. He is young, believed to be aged between eighteen and thirty. He is tall and described as gaunt. On the day in question, he was wearing a red T-shirt and navy jeans. In the sketch he looks ethereal; his eyes, with their white irises, have a shallow, insect look to them. Adrian murmurs, "He looks like a ghost."

"Shush!" says Beattie.

Police hope to speak to this man.

The Metford children have been missing since Sunday afternoon—for more than twenty-four hours. The police are requesting that anyone with any information contact them—they put up a number that can be rung. When the report is finished and the newscaster comes back on the screen, his lips are pressed together by the seriousness of the thing.

The clink of the spoon against the rim of the bowl makes Beattie glance at her grandson. Adrian is in his pajamas, his feet swaddled in fuzzy socks. A fastidious child, he hasn't spilled a drop of the liquefied ice cream, nor has a spot of it gone astray on his chin. He looks very pale against the darkness of the leather, and he has stopped eating the dessert. He can be fretful, easily put off his food. It is one of the things that annoy her about him.

Adrian worries about all sorts of things. Many of his fears he keeps private, sensing that there's something a touch ludicrous about them, but that does not lessen their power. He is afraid of quicksand—scared that one day he'll be walking along the street and find that the footpath is gobbling him down. He's heard about quicksand on TV and read about it in his grandfather's collection of *National Geographic,* the magazines a source of untold marvels and menace. In the streets he never sees any signs alerting pedestrians to the presence of the treacherous glug, and he worries that he won't discover for himself what it looks like until it is way too late.

Naturally he dislikes seeing his closet door ajar, especially at night, especially when he knows that when he last saw it, the door was closed.

Spontaneous combustion worries him. He knows enough to know there's nothing one can do to avoid it—it's pointless, for instance, seeking the shade on a hot day, or keeping some distance from the gas stove, in the hope that this will ward off the smoking fate. If one is programmed to self-combust, it's going to happen eventually, regardless. It's like being born with six fingers, a curse.

Tidal waves are another thing. Adrian doesn't spend much time at the beach, but the concern is there. He envisages himself sucked far out to sea by the retreat of a great wave, bobbing helplessly among umbrellas and bottles of sunscreen. He thinks of the water not yet risen into the wave, swirling, scheming, passing the time, in the pits of the ocean, restive as blood.

And now there are sea monsters, of course.

Others of his fears are more personal; they touch his heart like a needle through his skin. If he is in a shopping center with Beattie and the alarm rings for closing time, he is almost frantic to drag her out the door. The idea of being locked inside a shopping center fills him with absolute horror. He dreads and distrusts crowds, and amid them his one aim is to prevent himself getting lost. To be lost in a crowd would, he thinks, be like being buried alive. His father had once taken him to a carnival that was dazzling with color and fumes and bustle and noise; he'd been given a ball of cotton candy and patted a Clydesdale's satin hide, but Adrian's strongest recollection is of the sweat that slicked his father's fingers as he clutched the man's hand in his own.

He worries that one day his grandmother will forget to pick him up from school. He thinks he could walk home if he had to, though the walk would take a long time, but when he tries to travel the route in his head, the streets twine and mingle like spaghetti in a can, disorienting him in his chair. Each time the school bell signals the end of another day, he feels a chill down his spine: maybe today is the day. To be lost or forgotten or abandoned and alone are, to Adrian, terrors more carnivorous than any midnight monster lurking underneath a bed.

And now there is this new fear, one that settles so comfortably among its myriad kin that it seems familiar, as if it's skulked there, scarcely noticed, all along. He does not know those Metford children, but they are children just like him, just like the children he sees every day at school. On the TV, in the Metford yard, he had glimpsed a black-and-white striped basketball exactly the same as his own. He does not recognize their street, though it's only twenty minutes' drive away, but he feels as though he has seen it before. The trees, the fences, the rooftops, the clotheslines—that is middle-class suburbia, and Adrian is a suburban boy. He has been to the birthday parties of his classmates, and he knows that most things everywhere are more or less the same. A cat that strolls along the fence, a clock that ticks on the kitchen wall, finger paintings magneted to the fridge, side tables marked with coffee-mug rings.

It has never occurred to him—and he blushes faintly, for being so stupid—to think that children can vanish. The Metfords have not been lost or abandoned—they have been made to disappear. They have not run away— they have been lifted up and carried. They've been taken somewhere as distant as Jupiter. Adrian has never thought that an ordinary child, a kid like himself or Clinton or that freckle-nosed girl, might be of interest to anyone except family and friends, that an ordinary child could be worth taking or wanting, a desirable thing.

He stands at the wide living-room window, which overlooks the steep slope of the front yard. In the center of the lawn is a liquidambar that's losing its leaves. Along the fence are the thorny remains of Grandpa's roses. There are lots of roses planted in the neighborhood's gardens, for most of the people who live nearby are ancient, or at least seem so to Adrian—he thinks of roses as flowers of the elderly, coral pink, waxy cream, blowzy crimson. His grandmother's house stands high at the junction of a T intersection, and the house frowns down the stubby stalk of the T. In the smoky twilight, Adrian can see only shadows of what lies down there—a great expanse of little-used parkland and, beyond that, the local swimming pool enclosed behind cyclone wire. The crossbar of the T curves at both ends like a pair of bull's horns, the road sweeping around the shape of the hill. This makes it difficult to see the neighboring houses, and Adrian sometimes imagines that his home sits by itself on the hillside, solitary as a ship on the sea. The parkland is as murkishly green as any weedy ocean. Only one thing spoils this flight of his imagination, and that is the existence of the two houses that stand across the street, in the armpits of the T, the only houses, of the thousands that surround him, that Adrian can easily see.

Both houses are owned by one man, though they're separated by the road. Mr. Jeremio lives in the smaller and older house, and he spent five years toiling to build the grander and uglier of the two. The new house hulks up from its concreted land, two stories of plasma-yellow brick. Although it is supposed to be finished now, to Adrian's artistic eye the house looks somehow incomplete. It looks, to him, in desperate need of cleaning, or decorating, or *grace*—like a doll to whom the manufacturers have forgotten to give hair. But Mr. Jeremio is proud of it and thinks it's beautiful, and that, says Gran, is what matters.

Adrian stands at the window, gazing through the venetian blinds, but his hand has crept up, to the full reach of his arm, and his fingers have hunted in the air until they've come to rest on the cool swayed back of a cherub. The cherub, sitting perkily upright on its knees, forms a handle for the lid of an antique ornamental bronze bowl that occupies the end of the mantelpiece and generally goes unadmired. Adrian, however, loves it—he has inherited his grandfather's baroque taste. He loves the curvaceous shape of the bowl, its fruity heft and mossy color. He loves its frieze of wildflowers and its four spindly clawed legs. The lid fits the bowl with a precision

31

that utterly satisfies. The cherub, with its know-all leer, is less angelic than bacchanal, less endearing than jeering brat. It is chubby, every part of it convex, hoping to look tender and vulnerable when it is in truth hard and cold. Three fingertips fit nicely around the *putto*'s tombola-sized head, and its chin is polished from years of being thus grasped to lift the lid, but when Adrian pincers its ears between his fingers, he imagines the cherub's shrieks of insulted rage. Of all the things in his grandmother's house, his favorite is this cocky angel on a bowl. It pleases him just to see it, to sniff its archaic aroma, to touch its patina hide.

With his other hand, he pushes the venetian slats a little farther apart, edging nearer to the foggy glass, his concentration caught on the big house across the road. Yesterday and always there was never light in its windows, but this evening light is there.

The sound of the door opening makes him jump backward, his hands huddling to his throat. But it is only his uncle, who smiles quickly at him. Rory is odd, sometimes he is unnerving, but he never accuses Adrian of being into mischief and probably would not care if he was. He is carrying a mug of water, which he puts down coasterless on the piano. Adrian watches him take from the lion-handled sideboard one of Gran's precious wine glasses. The glass is perfect, like a jewel ("I want to keep them that way, Adrian"). His uncle says, "Now listen."

He dips a finger in the water, shakes the drips onto the carpet, and puts the finger to the glass. He runs his fingertip around the rim, and in a moment Adrian hears it, a high thin wail that is hardly there, a sound like ghosts thinking, like the shimmer of sleet in the air. Adrian looks wide-eyed at his uncle, who lifts his dark eyebrows. The noise dips and crests and rings away as Rory's circling finger slows down. "You see?" he says. "Didn't I tell you? Crystal sings."

"Can I try?"

His uncle proffers the glass: Adrian dampens a fingertip and presses it to the rim. At first the glass is mute as a fish; then, like a dog, it begins to howl. Its song summons goblins and worms from the ground. Adrian smiles, handing the glass back to his uncle. "That's good," he says.

"Were you spying on the new neighbors?"

The boy quails slightly. "No. I didn't see anyone. Only light."

"There are people there, though."

Rory puts the glass aside, and Adrian follows him cautiously to the window. In the minutes that he's had his back turned, darkness has come down. Nevertheless, the pair of them peek through the blinds, Adrian at his uncle's elbow. They can hear, drifting from the den, the theme tune of *The Young Doctors,* Beattie's favorite program.

"Mr. Jeremio's finally rented out the house." Rory, home all day, has plenty of time to observe the happenings of the neighborhood, although he would not say that doing so particularly amuses him. "They spent all morning moving in."

"Who are they?"

"I don't know who, I only know what. There's a man, and there's some children."

The news doesn't please Adrian: he knows his grandmother will try to force an introduction and maybe even friendship, and Adrian's shy soul rebels. He asks, "What about a mother?"

"A mother I didn't see. The children were two little girls and a boy."

Adrian sniffs, rubs his eyes with a pajama sleeve. He is tired, and the information doesn't sink in. His uncle must stare down at him and say, "That's strange, don't you think?"

"What's strange?"

Rory sighs. "Concentrate, Adrian. Two girls and a little boy. Like those kids we saw on the telly."

To Adrian, Rory's reluctance to do anything except wander round the house is less a mystery than a fact of life—the boy knows his uncle's lifestyle is unusual, but it's never offended him. Adrian wants a calm and rosy world; he is prepared to accept anything, if anything is what keeps the peace. He isn't old enough to understand that not all lifestyles are deemed acceptable to live. Rory's sister Marta knows better—she is a woman who unfailingly knows better. Marta believes that her brother is doing nothing more dignified than malingering.

Only Beattie understands that Rory is hiding. Although her patience is tested by him, she understands that he stays indoors because if he went outside, he would blow away on the lightest breeze, so excavated is he.

Rory's father, just over one year dead, had been a prosperous accountant. He had known his spirited son would never join the family business, and indeed, when Rory finished school, he had taken on a job at a local liquor store. The young man had wanted money, a lot of it very fast, and his father, although wealthy, would give him none. The accountant knew that money shows its true worth only to those who earn it. But Rory thought his father tightfisted; he cultivated a grudge. He needed to show how much he despised every mundane principle that guided his father's life. He worked day and night until he'd saved enough to buy the most wasteful thing he could think of, the single item most likely to appall his father's utilitarian heart. On the day after his twenty-third birthday, Rory bought a mustard-brown, silver-spoked, walnut- and leather-trimmed MG convertible.

Though it had been bought as a vehicle of resentment, the MG was the most gorgeous object Rory ever owned.

The car was almost two weeks old when Rory drove it at breakneck speed into a traffic-light pole. The tall pole had shuddered, its three blinkered lights flickering above the driver's woozy head. Rory opened his eyes to see the bonnet of the MG, once as sleek and curved as the flank of a cat, snarling and torn as a dog in a fight. It was night, there were flashing lights, Rory was groggy but conscious, and for a minute he was alone. Once the minute passed, there'd be eyes staring into his, hands reaching out for him, urgent voices in his ear. But he had a minute in which to exist alone, to hear a great silence within roaring noise, to crane his pounding head sideways on the creaking bucket seat, bitten tongue sponging the split in his lip.

His lifelong friend David was belted into the passenger seat. His head had been thrown back by the impact, so his nose pointed up like an arrow. A streetlight poured a misty beam over the young man's face, which was unmarked, not even bruising. In David's eyes Rory saw vacant places where David used to be. His face was so bland and shallow that Rory thought of the white interior of an empty and discarded bird's egg. A cool wind rose, and he thought of the life his friend no longer had in front of him, the woman he would not marry, the children he would not carry across the road, the old age he would not endure.

Footsteps were hurrying to the hissing, spitting MG when Rory saw David's hand move spasmodically in his lap. David had only died on the inside.

His body would continue its outside work, breathing, pumping, squeezing, sighing. But still there would not be a wife, babies, old age. On the inside there would always be the whiteness of the empty eggshell.

Rory often thinks about his father these days—he misses David, but he misses his father more. His father had not been a cruel or petty or spiteful man, but he'd known, Rory suspects, what cruelty and petty spite can breed. To Rory they'd brought destruction and boundless waste. His friend, his father, himself; the future, the past.

His father lies under churned clay and soil. David lies under blankets that are dyed baby blue. Each day Rory asks forgiveness from both of them. He knows the accident had sped the cancer through his father's body, that his father was killed by the guilt he'd determined to carry. The crash had been, for the older man, a symbol of mistakes he had made.

With the death of Rory's father had come other victims—Beattie, Marta, Adrian's mother, Sookie, Adrian, all of these now missing a fraction of themselves. Rory often thinks about David's parents, growing sadly older as they nurse their inert son. The effects of what Rory did that night have sprayed out like acid rain.

There is no making amends for stealing life, but Rory has given up much of his own vitality, as if trying to even the score. He has no desire, now, to truly *live*—none to participate, none to appreciate. Two years have passed since the collision, although the time seems longer. Rory is not the person he once was, and it's getting harder to remember what that diminishing person was like.

Rory paints strange pictures now; he hears himself saying strange things. Occasionally he'll be rude or nasty, unable to help himself—sometimes people have difficulty getting along with him. Rory hears things, he imagines things, some days he sees things scrabbling on his flesh. He prefers not to go outside. Like David, he is dead below the skin. His innards have been gutted, slashed, pulled about. Inside his chest is a cavern, and dripping slabs of muscle hang from his ribs like meat from butcher's hooks. No one knows about this abattoir within his body—or maybe his mother does. No one except maybe Beattie knows that Rory needs to stay indoors watching the world through a window because when he steps outdoors, the meat hanging on his ribs swings and sorrows with the wind.

At school the children are told they must not talk to strangers on the street. They are told that if they ever feel frightened by what a stranger says or does, they must run immediately to a parent or teacher or neighbor or shop-keeper, to anyone that they trust. The children sit quietly in their chairs, memorizing these instructions. One frightened girl begins to cry.

Adrian tells Clinton there are tenants in Mr. Jeremio's house, but such news is singularly uninteresting to a nine-year-old boy: enthusiastically caught up in the day's soccer match, his teeth black with licorice, Clinton hardly listens. Adrian reddens, wishing he'd never said anything, wishing he could scratch the words out of the air. He feels sick with the thought that he has been boring. For long moments he dares not speak, staring intently at the ground.

All week the newspaper has nothing to say about the sea monster.

Every night on television, they show the scenes of the crime. They show the house the Metfords live in, the streets along which the children walked. The ice-cream shop has become famous. They show close-ups of the clothing and sketches of the Thin Man, the wanted man, the one with whom they wish to speak. Every night they ask for help. There's nothing new to show or say.

Aunt Marta comes over for dinner, as she does once every week. Adrian sits alone in the den while his aunt, uncle, and grandmother eat in the dining room. He hunkers close to the heater, its warmth radiating down his spine, playing idly with an old board game. It is a vaguely magical game in which a small plastic robot-man, when pointed at a question printed on the board, will swing around of its own accord and touch the corresponding answer with its wand. *What are the three pure primary colors? Red, blue, and yellow. Who carved the* Pietà? *Michelangelo (1475–1564, Rome, It.).* Adrian tests the robot-man's knowledge again and again, until it rocks unsteadily on its lead-weight base. *Which is the world's largest mammal?* Blue whale. *Who developed the theory of gravity?* Isaac Newton. Mostly he can't hear what the adults are saying, but sometimes Marta's voice comes shrilling down the hall. She is never laughing—rather, he senses she is being thwarted, that she is lodging sharp protest. If he happens to be in the kitchen helping himself to ice cream or to Beattie's raisin scones, he may hear his gran tell her daughter, "Quiet now, don't get fussed." Some nights, although not this night, Marta leaves in tears.

On Friday Adrian's teacher announces that the class will be having a substitute teacher for the next fortnight. She is coy as to why this is, but Clinton reliably knows.

41

Clinton's mother is on the school board—she is the kind of pushy parent every school principal dreads—and uncovered the truth weeks ago. The teacher is getting married and afterward going on a honeymoon ("*Someone* must have money," broadcasts Clinton's mum: "You're not going to Hawaii on a schoolteacher's wage"). Some of the girls devise a plan, and when the bell rings to mark the end of the day, they make their teacher sparkle-eyed by hooting and whistling and throwing dabs of colored paper into the air. Above their cheers can be heard the alarmed, piercing whinny of a horse.

That night on television three mannequins are shown dressed in clothes that match the ones the missing children wore. The mannequins stand rigid, casting angular shadows against a wall. Their faces are pretty but blank. The tallest one, Veronica's, wears orange trousers and a hand-knitted vest; the sleeve of the shirt is pulled up to expose, on the wrist, a tiny, inky, heart-shaped mole. The Zoe mannequin is wearing overalls on the bib of which is appliquéd a rampant purple kitten; the bare arms of the dummy look breakable, subjected to the cold. The last and shortest, Christopher, wears velour, a matching navy set, its feet encased inside a pair of stunted blue duck boots. The three mannequins are arranged side by side, and a tape measure, tacked to a wall, indicates their heights. Adrian is struck by their frozenness. The mannequins wear wigs of bulky fair hair and their skin is painted softly pink, their faces are dusted with makeup to give them color, and ivory teeth shine from between rosy lips, but still they look far from alive.

Three

The first time Adrian sees her she is bent weeping over a bird. His grandmother has sent him outside to play, though it's chilly and there has been rain—Gran seems to believe he'll start to smolder (*self-combust?*) if he stays indoors too long. He has noticed that she's never concerned by the hours he must spend locked inside a classroom, but he keeps her contradictions to himself. He puts on a parka and his hands into his pockets and trudges down the drive.

The park is as empty as ever. He wonders about its perpetual state of desertedness—it feels like a forsaken place, a rejected one. He wonders if everybody knows a terrible truth about this land that he alone has not been told. Other times he fancies he is the only person who's ever realized the park lies here, that he is a boy who knows where there's hidden treasure.

The park is enclosed by the backsides of houses, by the dead-ended stump of road, by the fence of the local swimming pool. It is thickly planted with trees around the edges, while the center is a broad grassy field. The wind sweeps the grass into rippling waves. The sunshine of the previous weekend had made the grass long and garish lime, and yesterday or the day before the parks department man has come to cut it. In summer, when the grass is dry, Adrian builds fragrant huts from armfuls of mown clippings; now, soggy with the beginnings of winter, the flecks of green stick to his jeans and clag in wads to the soles of his desert boots. Water squelches when he walks on the grass, threatening to soak through to his socks, so he sticks to the gravelly path that meanders along the outskirts of the trees and is dotted with little puddles, stamped with the paw prints of dogs.

He can feel how white the weather has made his face. The wind blowing against him is so cold that he can feel himself wearing his skin. Oddly, under his wild hair, Adrian's ears feel stinging hot. He will walk three times round the oblong path and then go home and tell his gran it has started to rain, whether or not it had. He is not scared—the park is as familiar to him as his bedroom, as the private space beneath his bed, and he knows that nothing bad can happen to him here. If the Thin Man came, Adrian would simply run, and he wonders why the missing children had not done the same. He isn't scared, but he's bored and cold, and the fresh air is hard to breathe.

Because he's walking with his eyes down, watching where he treads, he does not spot her until he is five or six paces away. Then, he gets such a surprise to see her that he's pushed backward a complete step. The girl is crouching on the path, and her hands are pressed to her face; before her, where the grass meets the gravel, huddles a small brown bird. The girl is unashamedly crying, making a sodden but hearty noise. Adrian's instinct is to flee, to turn on his heels and make a casual escape, pretending never to have noticed a thing. But the girl slides her hands from her cheeks and glares at him, and smears her nose with her sleeve. "You!" she says, aggressively accusing. "You have to help!"

He hesitates, blinking. He manages to ask, "What's wrong?"

"This bird is sick. We have to put it somewhere safe. A dog will get it, or someone will tread on it, if we leave it here."

She rocks on her haunches, her rucked coat lolling in the mud. Her face is florid and blotched with tears. She has long, jet-black hair that floats in an untidy frizz, and eyebrows like two parties of Indians coming to powwow across a plain. She is not at all pretty, although Adrian is at the age where appearance plays no part in his attitude toward girls. He is wary of them all. "You pick it up," she commands. "I'll show you where to put it."

He comes guardedly forward. The girl stands and steps away, swabbing her eyes with her coat hem. The bird is slumped against the gravel, wings folded loosely at its sides. The lids are drawn partway over its eyes. Closer, Adrian can see a ring of fluid around its head, a delicate ruby crown. It is breathing heavily enough to ruffle its soft breast feathers. "Pick it up!" the girl, behind him, snaps, making his heart jolt. "Be careful!"

Adrian takes his hands from his pockets, unfurling cramped fists. He slips his fingers beneath the bird's body and feels the legs, like craggy twigs. The creature has no weight when he lifts it; it's hard to believe it is cupped by

47

his hands. The girl strikes out across the grass, and he follows her into the urban forest, shielding the bird protectively. She is older and taller than he—Adrian supposes she is about eleven. By the trunk of a eucalypt she stops; at the foot of the tree there's a tangle of weeds that have been kept dry by the high canopy. She kneels to inspect the site, which evidently satisfies. "Put it here," she says. "It will be safe."

Adrian has not taken his eyes from the bird. Its head has sunk, the beak sliding between his fingers. It has flown away, leaving feathers and bones in his hands. He thinks it is amazing that it should die so gently, without a sound. A bird is noise, until the end. The girl is still smudging tears from her face, and he doesn't want to tell her. He lowers the creature carefully among the weeds, and its head sags to one side. He tries to straighten it with a finger, but the girl has already seen. "Oh," she says, "it's died."

"Maybe it's sleeping . . ."

"No, it's dead. Poor little thing."

Together they consider the corpse. Its feet are like mummified spiders. "Shall we bury it?" asks Adrian.

"Yes," says the girl, "we must."

They rummage for sticks to score the earth, which is

riddled with tough roots and stones and as pliable as concrete: it is hot work digging the shallowest pit and their teeth clamp with the effort, their fingers cramp round the sticks. Close to the girl, he can smell the shampoo in her hair. Finally she sits back and, with a formal nod, directs that the funeral may begin. Adrian lays the bird in its undersized grave; already there's an ant investigating the body. While he brushes dirt into place, the girl, fingers woven under her chin, chants an affecting prayer. "O bird," she says, "take your love to the sky. Fly with the angels and Odin and Thor. Wait up in Heaven for me. Remember your life and those who have loved you and fly, fly."

Adrian pats down the earth, which is serving its purpose imperfectly—flecks of brown feather show through. The girl shreds some grass and sprinkles it about, and soon the grave is well covered, camouflaged. The children stand, and Adrian recalls the cold; the girl has coaxed a sheen of tears into her eyes and now deals with it manfully, pinching her arm until the emotion is driven down. Adrian has never met anyone so impressive, and when she wanders back to the path, he creeps after her, feeling himself at her mercy, expecting to be summarily dismissed. She has dried her face and her cheeks are no longer so mottled, but her voice, when she speaks, is damp and without gruff. "It's a tragedy when a bird dies, don't you think?"

Adrian gazes up at her. "Uh-huh."

"Birds shouldn't have to suffer. They shouldn't have to do what everyone else does." She gives a ragged sigh and glances sideways at him. "Thank you for your help, whoever you are."

He says, "I'm Adrian."

"Adrian?" Her mouth twists. "That's a funny name. I've seen you in your garden. I live across the road from you."

He nods quickly. "In Mr. Jeremio's house."

"Is it?" She gives another fragile sigh. "I don't know."

"What's your name?"

"That's not your business. Nicole."

She starts to walk away, but he stays where he has stopped, unsure what she wants him to do. He suddenly feels the wind again, how numb his feet have grown. She is walking in the opposite direction from the one which would take them home. When she's ten strides down the path, she spins to look at him. She's wearing a poncho striped with a dozen colors; the stripes churn when she moves. "What's up there," she calls, "behind that fence?"

Above the treetops, high on a low hill, can be seen the silvery peaks of a wire fence. Adrian hurries to catch up to her. "It's the swimming pool. It's shut for winter."

"I want to look," declares Nicole.

The children leave the track and weave through the man-made forest. Where the trees are thick, no grass grows and the ground is brackeny: Adrian has found nests here and fallen fledglings, and once he found a dead rat. He peeks fleetingly at his companion, sensing she'll be offended if she catches him. From each of her dark eyebrows spreads a scattering of hairs that scout the way ahead. Rain from days earlier drips from the shaggy canopy, spattering their clothes. The land rises steeply and their shoes slide beneath them as they climb; their hands get grubby saving themselves. Finally they reach the top of the hill, where the trees abruptly give way and the wire fence rises to the sky. Nicole, breathing heavily as the bird had done, threads her fingers through the diamond-shaped holes. Before them, laid out tidily as a child's tea set, are the local swimming pools.

There are three pools, each a different size and depth. Surrounding them is an apron of concrete and manicured lawn. The kiddies' pool is shaped like a kidney. The middle pool is square. The last and biggest, the adults' pool, is

51

rectangular, with blocks at one end for diving. The two smaller pools have been drained for the off-season, and their tiled walls glint with the rain. The big pool wears the blue cover that is its winter coat. The cover is in four pieces, each of the pieces laced with rope to the sides of the pool and laced to one another, too, so the giant pieces fit with hardly a gap—just a bead of wetness escapes the joins. The cover lies flat and still, like a shell of thick ice. It is hard to believe there is water below.

On the distant side of the lawn are the kiosk and changing rooms. There are tall metal umbrellas and some topiary shrubs, but no trees. There's a concrete cactus for children to climb, and high poles to which megaphones are attached. In summer the voice of the pool attendant barks orders across the suburb. *No running, no dunking, no bombing, a locker key has been found.*

Adrian stands beside his neighbor, the wire biting into his forehead. Nicole stares in silence while she catches her breath. She tilts her chin to see the top of the fence, squinting at the washed-out sky. "We could climb over," she suggests.

Alarmed, he yelps, "Don't!"

She holds tight to the fence and leans back on her

heels, and the wire bounces her. The wind is impossibly colder on top of the hill, licking the chill off the concrete and tiles. Nicole is smiling, contemplating the crime, and to distract her he asks, "Do you go to school?"

She looks at him as if he's mad. "Of course I go to school!"

"Which one?"

He thinks she might have enrolled at his own, as it is one of the nearest. But Nicole only says, "It's none of your business."

He ducks, embarrassed. She seems infinitely older and smarter than he—he wonders if he will ever understand what is and isn't anyone's business. Tentatively he tries again, asking something he already knows so it won't matter if she does not deign to reply, he'll still have some sort of victory. "Do you have brothers and sisters?"

"What's it to you?" She glowers from beneath the eyebrows. "Do you have any?"

". . . No."

"Then why are you asking me if I do?"

Adrian swallows; for a dreadful moment he thinks he's going to cry. He feels, again, the weightlessness of the bird, its velvety chest feathers. "I have to go home," he whispers.

53

"All right, go."

He turns and picks his way down the hill, using the eucalypt trunks to stabilize his journey. As he steps out onto safe flat land, he hears, from above him, "Thank you for caring about my bird."

Beattie, in the kitchen, suddenly thinks of the Thin Man. She has sent Adrian outside to play, and he has been, since then, very quiet; it's an instant that squeezes the air from her lungs when she realizes he's gone not into the garden, as she had intended, but across the street to the park. Adrian is alone in the park, and the Thin Man is on the prowl.

She rushes to the front door, flour clouding from her. She sees him snatched, broken, killed. She hasn't felt such terror since her own children were young—since the police knocked with news of Rory's accident—but it's a terror as recognizable as her reflection. She flies through the door and out to the veranda, which offers a view of rooftops for miles. Immediately she sees him, drifting along the footpath with his hands in his parka pockets, and even as painful relief fills her she thinks of the damage he's doing to the pockets' stitching, she feels the stretching of seams. Driven by forces beyond her control she rushes down the steps and across the garden, and when Adrian sees her charging toward him he's so startled that he does not move. She grabs him by the hood of the parka and shakes him, swatting at his head. She is not old, and she's strong, and she hits hard enough to know he'll be hurt. "I told you not to go to the park!" she shrieks, aware she said no such thing. She shakes and batters him regardless, wanting him to share her fear. Adrian flails; he is shaken out of his parka and falls to his knees on the lawn. He cringes, and she looks down at him—down and down, as if she's grown to be a giant. Mud is flecked across his nose; he is blinking frightened gray eyes. The whites of his eyes are so stainless that they are almost blue. She's furious enough to kick him, repentant enough to howl. "Inside!" she splutters. "Inside with you!"

He is on his feet and haring up the drive. Beattie wipes her palms on her apron, wringing her fingers. She glances around the street, hoping no one has witnessed this spectacle. It is undignified to raise one's voice in public, the kind of thing a fishwife would do. The neighboring houses are full of the elderly, most of whom have nothing better to do than pry and spread gossip like a virus. Her hand smarts from thumping his skull. She notes the cold breeze and looks up at the sky. Soon it will rain. It was time he came in.

She crosses the lawn, dampness rising around each step. She had not meant to be so rough on him—she had meant to be relieved. But what she feels is sometimes hard for her to express—she was brought up to despise weakness. Much of what is best in her is warped on the voyage from within to without. Concern emerges disguised as cruel rage and breeds a corrosive, truculent remorse. She will not ever say sorry. As she plods on leaden legs back to the house, Beattie acknowledges yet again that, although still young, she is too old and tired to be bringing up a child.

On Monday the substitute teacher is waiting for them. She's older than their regular teacher, and much more disturbing. She points to a child at random and shouts out a word to be spelled. Adrian quavers over *tomato*, is staggered to get it right. When one boy's attention dawdles, she smacks a ruler on his fingertips to hurry it along.

"What's this?" she asks, dangling Horsegirl's bridle like a repellent rag.

"It's mine!" Horsegirl snarls, baring a trapdoor of teeth. Adrian, for a flicker, is reminded of Nicole, her temper. He has scoured the school yard in a futile search for his neighbor. Meanwhile, the other children are coming to Horsegirl's aid, driven less by sympathy than by dread of a scene. "She's allowed to have her reins," babbles the most motherly of the girls. "Our proper teacher lets her."

The disgusted tyrant seems unconvinced, but she drops the reins over the back of Horsegirl's chair, from where they slide gracefully to the floor. "Leave it!" she brays, as Horsegirl bends to fetch them. "They're perfectly safe there."

Horsegirl straightens in her seat, pink-faced, muttering demonically. She chews her knuckles and cracks them.

At lunchtime Adrian takes his pocket money to the snack shop and buys a Wizz Fizz. He doesn't see the tiny spoon and tarries in the undercroft, poking around in the sherbet, disappointed. When he eventually arrives back at the haunt by the restrooms, Clinton is no longer there. Adrian stares across the playground, forgetting the missing spoon, and spots his best friend on the far side of the yard. He is deep in conversation with the lanky scholar of their grade, Paul. Another child might have run to join them, but Adrian lingers where he stands. Self-conscious, reserved, he feels a miserable foreboding. Rather than lurk unwanted on the edge of the discussion, he sits against the bricks to wait and does his best to appear intensely involved in every speck of sherbet.

That week, at school, small changes are made. Playground duty is done not by one teacher, but two. At the end of each day, there are more mothers than usual waiting at the gate — a nun comes to collect the children of St. Jonah's. Siblings gang together before embarking on the walk home. Kids on banana-seat bikes ride side by side. The children are told they must look out for one another. Many of them have already forgotten why.

They put the parents on television. People look up from what they are doing to watch, silent. It is as if a hush drapes over the world, as if monumental anguish smothers sound. The two sit at a plain table, and flashbulbs flare against their faces. The mother's skin looks tissue-thin; she has holes where her eyes have been.

"Please," she says. "Please, please." It's as if she has forgotten having other words.

The father clutches her hand so hard it must ache. He doesn't look doughy now, but taut; his eyes are jumping from flash to flash; he has the look of an anxious cat. He bends close to the microphone that sits on the table pointing reproachfully at him. "We don't care who you are," he splutters. "We don't want anything to happen to you. We only want the children. Just—let them go, let them walk away."

The mother says, "My loves . . ."

"They're good kids," says the father. He is grappling with something unseen, reasoning with the unreasonable. "We miss them. We want them home."

The mother moans, "Have mercy . . ."

"There's something suspicious about the father." Beattie is standing at the den's door holding Adrian's bowl of ice cream. Rory glances at her. He has sat all day in the same chair. He has not yet switched on the lamp, and darkness has gathered in the corners of the room. The TV throws a multicolored sheen across his face.

"You think he took his own kids?"

Beattie sticks stubbornly to her guns. "He's strange."

Her son scoffs dismissively and turns back to the screen. The warm light of the radiator makes his curls

59

look like rich chestnuts in a bowl. "Maybe having all your kids abducted turns you peculiar."

The mother says "Please" one last time, as though repetition is the key. The television cuts away to images of the children. Veronica, Zoe, Christopher—they are becoming as recognizable as friends. A policeman is shown saying that vigilantes will not be tolerated. Then the newscaster appears, introducing a warehouse fire. A week and a half after their disappearance, the Metford children are the lead news item only if there's something new-minted to say. They are slipping away, and the mourning parents cling to the edge of the table as if struggling to halt the slide. Beattie crosses the room and sets the bowl on the carpet beside Adrian's knee. "Dinner's served," she tells Rory, and leaves the room.

"What's a vigilante?" Adrian asks his uncle.

"A rabid dog." Rory levers himself from the grip of the chair and shambles into the hall. Adrian sees slavering hounds on the streets, their jagged yellow fangs. He picks up the bowl and begins to mash the ice cream with the spoon. He keeps hearing, in his mind, the mother saying *please*. He remembers the tragic cat-face of the father. Their loss is eroding them; they seemed only as solid as paper. Adrian thinks of the dying bird, how insubstantial it had been. If they can't get their children back, then the parents are likewise destined to vanish, just empty skins left behind, walking, talking, breathing, hollow. Veronica, Zoe, Christopher: it seems foreign and amazing, to Adrian, to think that someone might need someone else so very very much.

Four

He stands before his grandmother's dressing table, wincing intermittently as the comb drags through his hair. The crystal-backed brush and mirror glimmer enticingly, but he doesn't reach for them. In his hand is folded a shiny red plastic disk that's designed to clamp to the spokes of a bicycle wheel and lend some decoration. At breakfast Adrian had fished in the newly opened box of cereal, plucking the disk from the crumbly depths. He doesn't have a bike, but Clinton does. Adrian had hoped to retrieve, from the cereal, a toy or gadget for himself, but the spoke tag is good enough. As a gift, it will fix Clinton's friendship more firmly to the ground.

"Head up, Adrian."

He lifts his chin, scowling. In the dresser mirror he's projected back at himself, uniformed for school, his grandmother fussing over him, harried. She wields the comb as though it is a plow—he feels like he's being scalped. He watches her thick arm's reflection chop up and down as if working a hatchet. His sharp young eyes see wattles of skin wobble at her throat. His gaze wanders beyond her, into the glassy replica of the room. Behind his grandmother, tidily made, is the bed in which Adrian's grandfather died. He wonders how she can bear it, sleeping where a dead man lay. Simply being in the room gives Adrian the heebies.

His memories of his grandpa are sparse, and daily sparser. He has a muzzy recollection of his mother, Sookie, laughing at something the old man had said; he has another of standing by the bed looking down at the dying man and his father telling him he needn't kiss the pallid face if he didn't want to. He remembers Saturday newspapers spread across the kitchen table and the *whoosh* of the plane gliding down a length of wood; he remembers best the black mole on his grandfather's forehead that, when pressed with a thumb, would cause the gentleman to utter a sonorous *beep*. No matter how enthusiastically Adrian applied his thumb, the grandfather had never tired of the beeping, and neither had the grandson.

"Stand still, Adrian."

It is physically impossible to stand any stiller than he's doing, given that the grooming buffets like a gale. He spreads his feet as if the floor below him is a roiling sea. Watching his grandmother, he remembers his grandpa's funeral. There had been a lot of people in the church—most of them were old. The long mahogany casket stood on a delicate skeleton of steel. The casket lid was open, but from a distance all Adrian could see of the interior was the pleated ivory lining. His gran had taken his hand and led him past the pews, down the aisle, closer.

Peering over the wall of the casket, Adrian had been relieved to find his grandfather looking harmless. He didn't, of course, look anything like a living man, but neither did he look like something filled with the inexplicable darkness of death. He looked only like something whose existence was done. He'd looked, Adrian realized with some surprise, content. He had slipped his hand from his grandmother's grip and reached out to touch the mole. His grandpa's skin was completely cold. The instant Adrian's thumb pressed down, his grandfather bolted upright in the casket. His eyes flung open, his head jerked sideways, the face had leered at him. *"Beep!"* the corpse had screeched. *"Beep! Beep!"*

"There, you're done. Have you brushed your teeth?"

Adrian glances up, his imagination romping off like a pup. "Not yet."

"Well, get a move on. I'll meet you in the car."

He scrubs his teeth, grabs his bag, runs through the house and down the driveway without letting go of the red spoke tag. This morning his gran's maneuvering of the tank is faulty from the moment she exits the garage, and the vehicle must be driven forward and straightened four aggravating times. Adrian waits on the footpath, dampening in the morning drizzle. He can hear his grandmother's frustrated squawks as the car veers insistently for the house. He shuffles about, chilled and faintly panicked—the vehicle misbehaving inevitably summons forth Grandmonster. A sound from beyond his shoulder makes him turn, his jaw trembling with the shivers. Across the road, in the concreted yard of Mr. Jeremio's handmade house, stands Nicole. Bustling around her are a younger girl, a tiny boy, and a tall man. The man is directing the children into the rear seat of a car, the wide flat muzzle of which has not yet emerged from the garage, reluctant to greet the day. The smaller girl and the boy have the same flyaway black hair as Nicole; the man is nearly bald. Both the girls are carrying a rucksack, but they aren't wearing school uniforms—rather, they're wearing bright weekend clothes, as if none of their days are serious ones. Adrian waves, and Nicole, who's frowning over the fence at him, lifts a solemn hand. The man says something to her and she swings away, climbing quickly into the car. Adrian glimpses white as the soles of her sneakers disappear. The tank eases alongside him, billowing vapor, and he hauls open the slab of door.

Marta comes over for dinner, her weekly ritual. She has lived away from home, sharing an apartment with a friend, for the past couple of years. There is something about her visits that feels like an inspection. Beattie always sets the table with her best linen and silverware. She and Rory typically eat at the speckled Formica table in the kitchen; when Marta visits, the three of them eat in the dining room, the flames of two uneven candles pulsing in their eyes. On these nights, Beattie worries about her cooking in a way she never did when Marta lived at home.

Marta isn't the girl Beattie raised. That girl had been named Maggie. Marta emerged when Maggie turned twenty, announced that *Maggie* wasn't fitting, and rechristened herself with the new name. Marta gets terribly upset if Beattie forgets to whom it is she's speaking. In fact, there's a great deal about Maggie's mother, her siblings, and her history that upsets Marta, and she's been known to fiddle with the truth about each of these when in conversation with her glamorous friends—Marta has, on occasion, publicly denied she has any connection at all to this staid suburb and these unexceptional people. She has, just to be safe, thrown off most of those old companions who could catch her out in a lie. Now she's saying, "I told you, Mum. Didn't I tell you? I always said you'd regret it."

Rory sits at one end of the table, an elbow creasing the damask and his chin in his palm. He is not a big eater and has left most of the roast. Brother and sister do not get along and never really have, and they are now in the midst of a time-honored battle, a discussion that is served up at this table as frequently as gravy. It is a meaningless tussle, achieving nothing and going nowhere: Beattie brushes it like salt from her lap, forgetting as she hears. It is now Rory's moment to inquire archly, "What was she *supposed* to do?"

Marta is always spoiling for a fight, even for one as

senseless as this. She snarls, "Well, she certainly couldn't ask *you* for help. A *baby* can't care for a child."

It's another of those things Marta is loath to tell her smart friends, that her brother has evidently lost most of his mind. To her friends she describes Rory as eccentric; to his face she calls him a hypochondriac. Beattie won't stand for that, and here moves in to deflect the conversation back to the topic. She is keeping one ear tuned for sounds of Adrian nosing round the door—she can hear the gabble of the television and hopes it is keeping him hypnotized with some inanity. "Keep your voices down," she murmurs, reaching over the table to needlessly rearrange the serving bowls. "There are bat ears in the house."

Marta trembles, draws a persecuted breath. "I know you think I should take him," she says, "but think about it reasonably, Mum. He wouldn't fit into my life. And I refuse—I absolutely *refuse*—to be the dumping ground for other people's mistakes. Why *should* I be?"

"Yeah, why should you be?" Rory stares blackly down the table. "Why should you do anything for anyone?"

"Until you can make *yourself* useful, Rory, stay out of this!"

"Shh, now . . ."

"He's no trouble to keep, you know. He's docile. It'd be like having a Pekingese. You could fit one of those into your life, couldn't you?"

"At least I *have* a life!"

"Ignore him, Marta—"

"He's deliberately antagonizing me, Mum!"

Beattie ruefully shakes her head. She knows that her daughter leads a ritzy existence, that she has countless friends clamoring for her attention, that she's forever being invited to some exhibition or premiere. She has a job in advertising that involves long lunches, harmless flirting, and a sound knowledge of wines. It is a life like a maelstrom of all things material, modish, faddish, covetable, a life in which there's clearly no place for a somber nine-year-old boy—yet Beattie feels equally that there's no such place in her own. She has no youth left to give the young. Her husband had taken years to die, his cancer ponderous as a mule though leaving devastation in its wake; in the final year it had moved more swiftly, and also more gruesomely. In the drawn-out years of his dying, some of Beattie too had died: the husband's disease had chewed a dark path into the heart of the wife. Lester had become less a man than a burden to her; her fondest memories became infected, and love deteriorated into impatience and pity. With his death she believed herself freed—then Adrian had arrived, needy as a chick, remaining to hang like shackles from her arms.

The three of them contemplate their pale, smeared plates. In the background the television burbles away reliably. "If his own mother wasn't so hopeless," remarks Marta, pointlessly.

"And his father," adds Beattie. "Don't forget that fool."

"Both of them. So selfish."

"It's in the blood," says Rory.

Marta jabs like an adder. "Talking about yourself again?"

Beattie leaves them to it while she gathers up the plates. She deludes herself that they're fond of each other, brother and sister, though they've fought like curs since childhood. Only poor Sookie, the eldest, ever seemed glad for the comfort of siblings. Sookie always said that Maggie—*Marta*—could never forgive Rory for being born, for thieving the post of youngest and forcing her to become troubled middle child; the irony is that it's Sookie who is alone now, Sookie unforgiven and unseen. Piling the dirty plates on the sink, Beattie feels a surge of grief for them, her three marred children, beyond her reach and adult now, sunk so sightlessly into themselves that not one of them is capable of caring for any other thing.

Adrian stands at the living-room window. His fingers feel their way down the sleek body of the cherub, slowly and blindly as snails. A conscientious boy, he usually does his homework as soon as he gets in from school; this afternoon he is too restless, and his satchel lies discarded on his bedroom floor. He stares between the venetian slats, watching the wind toss the trees; distantly he detects Aunt Marta's perfume, an abrasive odor loitering in the dining room from her visit the night before. But he gives little thought to the scent or to what he sees: his concentration is all in his fingertips, in the cold solace of the bronze cherub, in its compact, bloodless permanence.

Adrian is a child for whom life easily falls apart. The smallest difficulties and upsets can effortlessly shatter him. Standing at the window, he is engulfed by worries that surge in sickening waves; his gray eyes have gone shiningly damp, as though the fears are leaking out. He is only nine years old, and already the world is overwhelming; he wonders how he will survive when he's grown, when his anxieties have had years to flourish and multiply.

Today, at school, Horsegirl has Gone Too Far. For the past week she has cultivated a hatred of the substitute teacher, and today she let it loose. Prickles run down Adrian's spine just to think about it.

All week Horsegirl has been less horse than some other, more capricious animal. She has sat at her corner desk and grizzled and gnashed and groaned. She has hissed, open-mouthed, tongue arching behind her teeth. She's thrashed her head, torn her hair, writhed her arms and legs. She has occasionally howled and gargled; one alarming afternoon she took to screeching like a cockatoo. The wild creatures inside her have fought one another in their determination to have their say. The substitute teacher has been the unnerved object of their derision. From the corner, every day, Horsegirl's feral grunts and yowls have greeted everything the teacher said and did. Today, this afternoon, it became more than anyone could bear.

Horsegirl had jibbered like an ape. She had joggled around in her chair. As the teacher talked of triangles, Horsegirl joggled, jibbered, and smacked her head in a hideous running commentary. Outside, the sky was colorless; rain was hammering down. The teacher's voice was high and strained. The children had long since stopped learning; they'd long since ceased to smirk behind their hands. Now they sat in rigid silence, swamped by Horsegirl and the rain and the tense, harrowed voice struggling across the room. Into the pits of their stomachs had seeped a pool of dismay. All of them sensed that nothing good would come of this.

None of them, however, guessed what was going to happen next.

The teacher snapped—like a rubber band, painfully. She stormed the length of the classroom, knocking pencils and books from the desks she swept past. She reached Horsegirl's table with her cheeks burning red. "Shut up!" she shouted. "Be quiet!"

Horsegirl, unflinching, sneered at her, spit blurting out her lips. Her hands fluttered above her head like broken, starving doves. She rolled her eyes, made choking sounds. The teacher thumped the desk. "Stop it!" she bawled. "Shut your mouth!"

Horsegirl's eyes stopped rolling with a jolt; her head lurched forward on her spindly neck and she yelled, a warped echo, *"Shut your own mouth!"*

The teacher's angry hand closed over Horsegirl's bridle, which lay draped along the edge of the desk. The child squealed in protest, lunging for the precious leather.

For a moment the bridle was pulled tight between them, buckles spinning in the air. Then Horsegirl screamed, and the teacher let go. "All right," the woman started, "sit down—"

But Horsegirl stayed screaming: her arm lashed, bull-whipping the long reins through the air. They slapped across the teacher's face, flipping up a hank of her hair. The sound of it was clean and spry: the little girl sitting behind Adrian gulped, horrified. The rain came down suddenly cyclonic, as if wanting this scene washed away.

The teacher put a palm to her cheek, rocking in her sensible shoes. She stumbled backward until she bumped a chair. Then she pivoted, bent double, and ran from the room. The children that she passed on the way would testify to her face being striped crimson, and to tears pouring from her eyes.

Horsegirl sat down to arrange her tack.

The other children sagged stupefied in their chairs. They gazed dazedly around themselves, rabbit-eyed. The absence of a teacher usually encouraged, from certain quarters, an uprising of chatter and mischief, but today even the naughtiest children had made no sound. All of them felt the ghastly wrongness of what had happened, that this was a thing beyond crime, beyond cardinal sin, to make a teacher cry. They understood they had witnessed something a child should never be allowed to see. Each of them felt they'd contributed in some way to this awfulness and that they would, in consequence, be resoundingly punished—each of them except Horsegirl, that is, who might have been oblivious but for the tight smile on her lips.

The little girl behind Adrian stood, and every pupil watched her wander the length of the room to where a waterless aquarium sat on a shelf. Inside the aquarium were silkworms, which the class was trying unsuccessfully to breed. The girl leaned her head against the glass, and two tears meandered down the pane. Adrian looked at Clinton, who sat alert as a hare. He would take this event home to his mother and return to school tomorrow with her opinion converted to gospel. Until that time, he would have nothing definite to say.

The classroom door had opened, and the principal came into the room. The children stood, as they'd been trained. "Sit down," she said gently, and they did. It was a relief to straighten their knees, to see a responsible face. She inquired of a reliable girl as to where the class was in its math book. "Finish the page," she told them. "I'll be back to see your work." Then she had left them alone again, and the feeling of discomfit had returned. Only

Horsegirl was calm and murmuring quietly, less carnivore than peaceable omnivore now. But Adrian had not doubted that she knew what she'd done, that some gleeful nook of her mind was obsessively rewinding and replaying the delirious scene.

The wind changed direction and threw hailstones at the windows. The weeping girl left the silkworms and stumbled back to her chair. The children flipped through their math books until they found the page. Finally, whispers had begun to rise. Paul, the clever boy, called out the first three answers, and everyone wrote them down.

Minutes later the substitute teacher returned. With her came the principal. The pupils stood, laying their pencils on the page. The teacher walked straight to the blackboard. The children she passed searched for red streaks. The principal went to Horsegirl's desk. Horsegirl was not standing and only unwillingly put her pencil down. The principal talked softly into her ear—Adrian heard her say Horsegirl's name. The child nodded and pushed out her chair. The entire class watched as she followed the principal from the room, slouching on her large feet, over-tall and ungainly, her dress ill-fitting, her face made for someone older. She had not forgotten to take the bridle with her and carried it tenderly, as though it were a kitten.

In the living room, Adrian's fingers are skirting the bowl. He feels the raised frieze of what are supposed to be flowers but have always looked, to him, like squashed flies. He stares through the rain-stained window, past the bare-boned liquidambar, and over the black span of road. It stopped raining an hour ago, but everything drips.

He had watched Horsegirl go, her head held high on a fearsome pride. He'd thought about the madness in her, a lunacy everyone knew was there, never guessing its frenzied depths. Horsegirl seemed to swim in her craziness; worse, she seemed to enjoy it. She was lawless and dangerous, frightening, repellent. No one could like her, no one wanted to talk to her or have anything to do with her, she was everything that was untouchable.

His fingers stagger around the frieze. He grazes his knuckles down the swollen flank of the bowl. Standing at his desk watching Horsegirl stalk away, his hands had craved the reassurance of the bowl, as though all hectic-ness could be stilled by its antique caress. His heart had pattered fast until the moment he'd pushed his palm to its gold-green side. Adrian does not know why, but every time Horsegirl's madness flares, he fears for the soundness of his own mind. He worries that what lives so violently within her is also living in him. He fears that Horsegirl is contagious, to nobody but him. He remembers his father once saying that Sookie, Adrian's mother, was mad; for good measure he'd added that Beattie, Rory, and Marta were mad too. He'd warned his son that, sharing as he did this unhinged blood, Adrian might well be crazy also. Adrian had known his father wasn't serious, that he was upset and being cruel, but nonetheless it bothers him, recalling those words. It's consolation to remember that Horsegirl is St. Jonah's child but that he, Adrian, is not: the difference is vast, vast enough to ensure they can never be the same.

Not long after she'd left the room, Horsegirl had returned. The children were astonished—not one of them had expected to ever see her again. But there she was, bringing her bridle and her mothy, wet-wool smell. She sat down and doodled the afternoon away, and the teacher didn't tell her to sit up, didn't ask her any questions or take any notice of her—though everyone in the classroom knew that she was there.

Adrian sighs. He lets his hand drop from the bowl,

and when he chews his thumbnail, his fingers smell bitterly of bronze. Today is Friday, and he is glad the weekend has arrived. Yesterday he'd presented the spoke decoration to Clinton, happy in anticipation of his friend's gratitude. Clinton, however, had glanced at the trinket and given it back to him. "I don't collect them anymore," he'd said—not unkindly, but the embarrassment made Adrian queasy. Paul, the smart boy, was standing nearby and asked to see the toy: when Adrian handed it over, Paul sent the disk flying like a miniature Frisbee. Adrian's nausea had stayed with him, and he'd wished his grandmother would let him miss a day of school. If he had been allowed to stay home today, he would not have had to see Horsegirl whip the substitute teacher.

But now it is the weekend and he's free.

Into the bare garden of the house across the road steps Nicole, trailed by her brother and sister. Adrian straightens, interested, pressing a venetian slat out of view. He lingers by the window long enough to ensure they're not about to go off in the car, then rushes for the front door. He runs down the grassy slope of front lawn, the fallen leaves of the ambar skittering in his wake. The chill of early evening scratches like cat claws; dirty water splashes his sneakers and the hems of his jeans. He's desperate to be with someone who played no part in the humiliation and bewilderments of yesterday and today.

Nicole and the children watch him run, craning their heads like birds. Mr. Jeremio built the fence low, with bricks the color of sour milk; along the top of them stretches an elaborate band of rusty-blue wrought iron that the builder has not bothered to paint. The four children grip the metal swirls, peering through the gaps at each other. Adrian's hair is in his eyes; the chilled air smarts his lungs. "Hello," he breathes, joyfully.

"What's your hurry?" snaps Nicole, but he can tell she is pleased. He hops up and down with cold and cheer, the winter at his chest like a cat, his fingers feeling frozen to the iron. He looks at the younger girl, who might be six, and at the boy, who is baby enough to drool. He resists an urge to reach between the metal twistings and pat the child's head. Excitement makes him babble— in one quick gulp he asks, "Where have you been? What have you been doing? Have you just been going to school?"

"Well, we—"

"Don't tell him, Joely!" Nicole clips her sister's shoulder and casts Adrian a lofty scowl. "Why are you always asking questions? How come you're always *why* this and *why* that?"

He shakes his head, bounces toes against the fence. "I don't know." And he really doesn't know, nor does he care what they say, so long as they continue to stand amiably at the fence with him and he can feel welcome. "What's your brother's name?"

"Giles," says Nicole, and the child looks inquiringly up at her. A skin of dribble has glazed his chin. Both Joely and Giles have hair like black lambs' fleece and their sister's shaggy sheep face. "He's only two years and six months," Nicole informs her neighbor, "so don't talk to him."

Adrian wiggles a hand through the serpentine iron, holding it out for Giles to sniff. The boy's cheeks are dewy and purpled with cold. "He's got a wet diaper," Joely warns.

Adrian hugs his hands to himself at this alarming news. "Maybe you should tell your mum?"

"No, she isn't—"

"I can fix it!" yips Nicole. "I'm not a *baby*, I can look after him. *You* might be a baby, but I'm not."

"I know you're not," Adrian hastens, in retreat. "I didn't mean—"

"What have *you* been doing, anyway?"

He blinks. "Nothing. Just going to school . . . Did you go to school today?"

His neighbor rolls her eyes skyward and drawls, "What do you reckon?"

Adrian shrugs, hopelessly confused. Joely is touching her nose with her tongue, chin tilted to the clouds. Giles gazes at nothing with the absent expression of the bored toddler; he balls a hand into his sister's palm and hangs his weight off it, sleepily closing his eyes. The ironwork contorts around the faces of the children, frames them with wrestling coils. The evening has come down heavily, a haze of pearly gray. Few cars travel this nowhere road, and the cold birds are all silent. Adrian comes cautiously forward, touching his wrists to iron. His lips and eyelids feel like icy wounds; his breath lingers under his nose. He hears himself asking, "Where did you come from?"

Nicole flicks an eyebrow. "From the moon."

Joely chuckles, liking this. "The moon," she chuffs. Giles continues to stand like a statue. Adrian smiles. "Where do you really come from?"

"I told you, the moon."

Joely snorts with mirth. "I come from the moon too," Adrian tries.

"Oh yeah? I never saw you there."

He bobs his head, knowing when he's defeated. "Will you stay on Earth forever?"

"Until we go to Heaven." It's a silly answer, but Adrian is satisfied; Nicole and Joely are giggling. A sound makes the three of them look around, laughter freezing in their eyes. The front door of Nicole's house has opened and a man is standing there. It's the same man who shooed Nicole into the car that morning she waved at Adrian. An arrow of wariness spears through him, and Adrian steps away from the fence.

"Inside," the man says flatly; he stares at Adrian as he speaks. "Come and eat."

The words could be an invitation, or command. Adrian takes blind backward steps to the gutter. Nicole hoists Giles to her hip and marches with Joely into the house; the door shuts behind them with a thump and clink of chain. It happens so quickly that Adrian is dazed to find himself alone in the dusk, standing in the gutter on the tips of his toes. He steps backward to the center of the road, considering the blank door and vacant yard; a moment moves slowly by before he turns and trots for home. From the corner of an eye, he glimpses the curtain sway in the bay window of the Jeremios' house—every street has its busybody, its lunatic-fringe dweller, and this street has Mrs. Jeremio. Adrian feels her eyes crawl like bugs on his back; he runs.

Five

There are, of course, many rumors going round. Most of them are absurd, and those who spread them feel vaguely ridiculous doing so. Nevertheless, the stories disperse, and there's horrible pleasure to be had in hearing something one hasn't heard before.

Inevitably, the first theory has a religious theme. The Metford family are members of a cult. Where cults are, there's sacrifice.

Quick on those unholy heels comes slavery. The children are gone, their identities scrubbed; there are blindfolds on their eyes.

It's said that the police are in daily communication with the Thin Man. The cops are receiving letters, hair, slivers of skin. There's talk of a ransom that the Metfords have been unable to meet. There's also rumor that bodies were found days ago, and that the continuing search and flashing of photos is a ruse meant to distract the public.

Another story, quick to surface, claims that Veronica, Zoe, and Christopher never existed—that they themselves are a hoax. There's a political aspect to this theory that is never satisfactorily explained.

There are alien abductions; there's ordinary old running-away-from-home.

No one believes a word of these tales. One night, on a railway bridge spanning a busy thoroughfare, four white words are painted in a dripping but steady hand: *Suffer the little children.* The following morning, three pink rosebuds bound by a white ribbon are left lying on the walkway below the bridge. From that day onward, the path grows into an alley of flowers.

Beattie takes Adrian shopping for clothes on Saturday, towing him by the hand through the bustling morning crowds. The boy clearly puts the excursion on a par with visiting the dentist, is unwilling and morose. Beattie, as she drags him, details how thrilled she would have been, as a girl, if her own mother had taken her to a lovely department store to buy dresses and bows and things. Adrian listens, but only because he can't avoid doing so. He remains steadfastly detached. When he does eventually see something that's slightly less tedious than everything else, Beattie is quick to find fault with his choice. She shames him by wrenching at stitching and scoffing at seams—"It's a waste of time looking for quality these days." She does not want him owning clothes that are merely fashionable—she can't afford to let him be like Clinton, indulged with everything he sees on TV. If she must buy clothes for a relentlessly growing child, they will at least be quality items that please her eye. Adrian, however, is unimpressed by sturdy buttons and generous hems. He wants a navy-blue duffel coat ("You want to dress like a wharf rat, is that right?"), but his grandmother knows his parka will suffice the rest of the winter. At the sight of his glum face, she scolds, "Stop being such a sad sack."

Rory has given his nephew a few dollars, and in the toy department the boy brightens considerably, deliberating over junky trinkets. "Buy a book," Beattie advises, but the suggestion fails to inspire. He scans the shelves of board games hungrily, running his fingers over the desirable boxes of Mouse Trap, Operation, and Ker-Plunk!, all of which are well beyond his meager financial reach. "Maybe for your birthday," Beattie consoles, though she knows it will be she who's forced to play the games with him, that she'll always prefer to be doing something else, that he'll grow quickly frustrated with her inability to remember the rules or to take the combat seriously. Finally he chooses a pile of metal, showing her how the coils can be poured like liquid from one hand to another, making as they do so a rather musical noise. "What do you call it?" she asks, and he chirps, "Slinky."

Slinky. Someone's making a fortune from factory off-cuts. When he's paid for and received the toy in a bag, she takes him to the store's cafeteria as a treat. From the array of desserts, she selects for herself a slice of lemon meringue pie. Adrian, who's inherited the McPhee sweet tooth, sets a bowl of chocolate mousse on his own plastic tray. They sit at a table by the mirror-lined wall, and while Beattie rummages through the things she's bought, he entertains himself by picking chocolate shavings from atop a blob of cream and sucking them down one by one.

He hardly bothers to look up when she unfolds his new sweater and admires the pattern cut in the velour.

Sitting at tables throughout the cafeteria are other grandparents having morning tea with other grandchildren. In most cases the children's mother is present too—the tabletop that separates Adrian and herself is as broad, Beattie muses, as a missing generation. Most of the grandparents won't be taking their grandchildren home with them—at any rate, not for keeps. Most of the grandmothers don't look into the future and see homework and hormones for years.

The meringue pie verges on being stale, but she will not complain. She'll put up with anything rather than complain. She was reared not to make a spectacle of herself. She glances into the mirrored wall and sees a creased face, snowy hair. Beattie is sixty, the wrong side of middle-aged; lately she has started dressing in the dowdy styles worn by her own mother in her declining years. Living with a child has not kept Beattie young—on the contrary, the past ten months have aged her disproportionately. She gives her reflection a wry smile, but she isn't amused.

She catches him studying her, big-eyed. "What's up with you?"

The boy smiles briefly. "You're making a noise."

"What? What?"

"When you chew." He hunkers in his seat. "You make a funny noise when you chew."

She slobbers her tongue over her gums horribly, and the child at once blushes and grows pale. "Boys who are nasty find their own way home," she tells him, and he glances whitely away. She watches him a minute, thinking it is strange—strange how love coexists with hate, how they render one another mute, how the swilling of them together makes a new and softer, sympathetic thing.

Still, she thinks, at least Adrian is well behaved. Looking around the restaurant, some of these brats she could throttle. Children nowadays aren't often taught about making a spectacle.

They leave the store before the bell rings to mark midday closing time, because she knows her grandson's fears. On the drive home he's in good spirits, the worst of the day being done. He is clearly pleased with his purchase of the Slinky, and when they arrive at the house, he runs inside to show it to Rory, abandoning the clothes in the car.

The afternoon is dry and warm, and he sprawls across the swinging lounge playing idly with the new toy. From the high front veranda, he has a view of the garden and the joint of the roads, but for much of the time, there's nothing worth seeing or watching. Eventually, however, the screen door of his neighbors' house opens and Joely rambles into the yard. She is carrying what seems to be a baby but proves, on closer inspection, to be a doll: she offers to let Adrian nurse it in exchange for a turn with the Slinky, an offer he cannot accept. But he hands the Slinky over and instructs her on its use, and they crouch side by side on the sunny driveway flipping the coils head over tail, tail over head. The light is speedy mercury that loops and loops the toy. Joely slides the coils along her arm, wearing them like bangles. She has stubby fingers, smells faintly of spilled food. "Are you always going to live here?" Adrian asks.

She screws up her lamblike face and laughs. "Have to live somewhere."

"You should stay," he says somberly.

Nicole interrupts them, barging from the house. She stands at the gate, arms folded. "What are you doing?"

"Nothing . . ."

"Look!" Joely shakes the Slinky so the coils rattle. Nicole marches nearer and takes the toy from her. Adrian watches uneasily as she bounces the spring up and down a few times.

"A girl at school has one of these."

He nods; then feels he must add, "I only got mine today."

"What will you swap for it?"

Adrian is taken aback. "I can't swap. My uncle bought it for me."

Nicole folds cross-legged onto the driveway, and the children crawl close to her. She reaches into the neck of her windbreaker and draws up a string of black leather. "What if I swap it for *this*?" she asks, supremely confident.

At the end of the string hangs a serrated white triangle. It wears a cap of silver and a shiny looping clasp. Joely gasps. "Not your shark's tooth!"

Nicole gives the tooth a tempting jiggle. Adrian feels its desirability like heat on his face. Clinton does not have a shark's tooth, although he'd dearly love one. Adrian hesitates, shielding the Slinky in his hands. "I don't know . . . I only got it today. It's brand-new."

Nicole narrows raven eyes. Her trousers have ridden up her calves, allowing a giddying glimpse of candy-striped socks. Joely hunches forward, deeply interested. Nicole darts a look at the Slinky. She thinks for a moment, licking her lips. She says, "What if I give you my Wombles yo-yo as well?"

Joely catches her breath, flabbergasted. Adrian, however, shies away. "Wombles are for girls!"

"They are not!"

"They *are*!"

Nicole looks sour, sunlight on her head. "Make up your mind!" she sniffs. "The Slinky for my yo-yo and my shark's tooth necklace. That's my final offer."

Adrian grimaces. The necklace is worth having. But the Slinky, too, is enviable; more than that, it's associated with the satisfaction of choosing for himself. "I don't think I should," he says. "My uncle will get angry."

Nicole screws up her face, disgusted, and returns the tooth to its hiding place. Joely offers, "I'll have your Wombles yo-yo if you don't want it, Nics."

"I *do* want it, stupid!"

Adrian has looked up, beyond his neighbor's shoulder. There is a woman striding purposefully along the footpath toward them, and everything in her manner says she will not walk right by. She is about to accost them, her expression determined, her jaw and fists clenched. Nicole notes his apprehension and twists to see what he sees; in the next moment the woman has swooped upon them.

She drops to her knees on the driveway, her arms encircling, her shadow spread wide; she comes down like a crane on the nest. "Don't be frightened," she whispers, her words hasty and rasped. "Don't be frightened now, you're safe—"

The children are more stunned than scared and duck from her clutches smiling uncertainly. The woman wears a nylon skirt, and Adrian hears the material crackle as it scrapes the concrete. Her arms grapple, wanting them closer, and the children squirm like worms. "Don't be scared," the woman murmurs, "I'm not going to hurt you. Tell me your names, little ones—"

Joely bites her lip and whimpers, pressed almost flat to the drive. Adrian tries to get to his feet, to escape the woman's overhang. He has realized who she is but cannot say the words. Meanwhile the woman keeps talking, and they're blown by soupy breath. The gold links around her throat flare warmly with the sun. "I'll take you to the police station; you'll all be safe there. Your mother will be so happy. Come, children, stand up, hurry—"

She grips Nicole's arm, and the girl lets out a wail. Joely immediately bursts into tears. The woman gives a frantic cry, her face creasing with concern. "Hush, hush, darlings! Don't you want to see your mother?"

"Camille!"

The voice comes from above them; Adrian, scrambling backward, sees his neighbor Mr. Jeremio. Typically a short man, he seems to have become broad-shouldered and huge. "Camille!" he repeats, gently stern.

The woman's hands, encompassing, hover in the air. She turns her head painstakingly, lifts her trembling chin. Her eyes curve into sad crescents at the sight of her husband. "Joseph," she says, "look who I've found."

Mr. Jeremio slowly shakes his head. Other days he's reminded Adrian of a sprightly squirrel; today, inexplicably, he is an old lion. "These girls are our tenants, Camille," he sighs. "Remember? Their papa rented the big house. And look—this is Adrian, from across the road. You know Adrian, don't you?"

Mrs. Jeremio sinks, her distant eyes sliding over the children. Adrian, Nicole, and Joely, bunched together on the concrete, gaze back at her tensely. Mrs. Jeremio's lips move, but it takes a moment for her voice to come out. "Yes," she breathes. "Adrian."

"These aren't the ones you're looking for, Camille."

"I know." She smiles nervously. "I know, I know."

"Their mother isn't worrying about them."

"No." She stands abruptly, brushing flecks from her

skirt; a waft of greasy perfume skates along the air. "Go inside now, children," she says. "You shouldn't be playing near the road."

Mr. Jeremio steps forward and takes his wife's elbow. He guides her to the footpath and leads her meekly away. The children perch on the drive and watch the couple leave. Shocked, none of them says anything—except for Joely's sniffing, they fail to make a sound. They watch while Mr. Jeremio guides his wife over the road and into the sanctuary of the house. When the door shuts behind them, Nicole spins to Adrian. "What?" she squawks. "What?"

"She didn't mean to scare us—"

"I wasn't scared!" the girl spits. "Who says I was scared?"

"She didn't know what she was saying, I think . . ."

Joely's tears overflow her eyes. "I want Mum . . ."

"You were scared, not me!"

"I want Mummy," Joely sobs.

Adrian shakes the Slinky, but the child puts her hands to her face and bawls. The driveway seems suddenly moist and uncomfortable, but they sag there as if lacking bones. "Joely wants her mum," Adrian acknowledges listlessly. "Where's her mum?"

"Where's *yours?*" Nicole leaps up, flinging wide her arms, her confusion solidified to rage. "You're always asking *why this, where's that?* Where's your own mum, stupid? We're not lost kids, you know!"

She grabs Joely by the scruff and yanks her to her feet; the child howls with terror as she's roughly hauled away. When the front door's kicked shut behind the girls, Adrian is alone. His teeth are imprinted along his lip. The sun is still shining, though a bank of pillowy clouds is drifting near. The Slinky capsizes as he gets stiffly to his feet. A stone has dug into his knee, and he picks it out with a fingernail. He hoists his trouser leg and sees that the stone has left behind the shape of itself buried in his skin.

Rory, in a fit of being unable to help himself, once said, "Adrian, your mother is as good as dead."

Adrian hadn't understood what his uncle meant—he could see nothing good about death or being dead—but nonetheless he caught the essence, the sense that something had gone very wrong in the life of his poor mother. He hasn't seen her since coming to live with his grandmother—she hadn't been at Grandpa's funeral, though everyone else had been there—because, Gran says, his mother isn't well. Gran says that it would be upsetting for Sookie if she were to see her son. Adrian doubts this is true. When he had lived with her, his mother never found the sight of him distressing. Occasionally she'd woken him in the depths of night only to tell him how much she loved him.

Adrian, however, is not completely ignorant. He knows why he's been taken from her. He doesn't like putting this reason into words; he dislikes making Sookie bear the blame.

Adrian had walked alone to his first school because his mother could never endure the world at that hour; sometimes when he came home, she'd been nowhere to be found. Some weeks there was no money for food shopping, and Adrian would eat honey bread. Sookie often slept on the couch, an ashtray at her elbow, and Adrian would curl on the carpet below her, watching TV and listening to her breathe.

His mother was rake-thin, as wide-eyed as an owl. She always had a cold and a headache. She could be emotional, scathing, suffocatingly fond. She lost patience with his childishness. She would rant against her family and against Adrian's father, counting off to Adrian their

98

blatant hypocrisies. She rarely took him anywhere—never to the drive-in or on a holiday—but he was content to stay home. She could be unpredictable and embarrassing, so he preferred it if she stayed home too. He never asked a friend to visit, although he would have liked to. Once there had been vomit in his mother's hair, and Adrian didn't want guests witnessing anything like that.

For all this, Sookie wasn't hopeless: bills got paid and clothes got washed and the house was acceptably clean. And Adrian adored her, for a mother must be much more dreadful than Sookie ever was before the affection of a child will curdle. None of this made any difference, however, when it was decided Adrian needed taking away.

It was no one real who decided this—it was an entity without a face, *authority*. Authority whispered behind his back, discussed him, laid plans. Adrian's father arrived, shoveling all the boy owned into garbage bags. "You brought this on yourself," the man told the woman, while Sookie sat and wept.

Your mother isn't well; the sight of you will upset her. Adrian is like a bird kept caged, perceiving that the truth is held from him. He knows he is told a tame and sterile version of what is actually true. Sookie isn't sick. And he doesn't believe that seeing him would upset her: rather, he thinks it would make her happy. For all his mother's faults, she had never made him feel unbeloved.

When the Metford children have been missing for exactly two weeks, there comes the unspoken realization that they are not coming home. Whatever has become of them, the hope is that it came quickly and painlessly, without too much fear. Whatever is being searched for now is not the same thing that was lost.

Rory watches footage of a police line shuffling across a boggy, grassy field. He wonders what they've been told to make them turn their attention here, to a patch of bedraggled wasteland bordered by factory walls. It is the kind of place one finds car tires and dead cats.

The ashtray wavers on the arm of the chair. The den is a compact room, wood-paneled, brown as a cave. There's a three-barred radiator set low in the wall and heavy paisley curtains in shades of copper and cocoa. The television hulks in a corner, encased in wood veneer. If this is a cave, Rory is a caveman, for this is his favorite room. The smoke of his cigarette whittles skyward as if from a campfire. This is the closest the young man ever gets to taking part in the great outdoors.

Rory will never shuffle through a grassy field. He won't feel pebbles beneath his boots. He won't slip in mud and soak his knee in a puddle. He won't, for balance, clamp a palm against a tree. He won't crimp his toes into beach sand or taste the salty splash of sea. Rain won't fall on his shoulders; snow will never freeze his ears. He won't stand in the shadow of boulders, nor reach the peaks of mountains. The sun won't blind him with its brightness, the wind won't pull his hair.

None of this will happen to the children, either.

Adrian is lying on the floor, propped on his elbows, waving his feet to some tune in his mind. He is drawing a picture on a clean white sheet, groaning quietly when the line goes wrong. He had looked up when the television showed the police search, but apparently had nothing to say. He looks up again now that the ads have come on, remarks, "They never show anything about the sea monster."

". . . What?"

"They never show anything about the sea monster." He glances over a shoulder at Rory, clearly aggrieved. "Remember the sea monster in the newspaper?"

Rory taps ash in the tray. "What about it?"

"It's never on the news. I've looked in the paper every

day, and it's never there, either . . ." He sighs, his nose crinkling. "You'd think people would be interested to hear about a sea monster, wouldn't you?"

"Maybe."

"I reckon they would. They should show it on the telly."

The child, disappointed, shakes his head. He brushes away strands of unkempt hair and returns to his work. Rory watches the fine lead marks take shape around a thing only visible to Adrian's eyes. There is concentration in every part of him, the hollow of his back, the slope of his shoulders, the flawless nape of his neck; even his feet have gone still, ceasing their private waltz. Watching him, Rory feels oddly as if he is prying. He wonders how the world looks from the viewpoint of a child, but does not manage to ask. Down the hall, in the kitchen, Beattie drops a pot and swears.

Six

Horsegirl is on the roof. Someone's noticed her and given a shout, and now the entire school is gathered at the base of the red brick wall, their chins tipped up as far as they'll go. Horsegirl is storming back and forth, snorting down at them. She is a high-strung thoroughbred, rolling eyes, tossing head, scraping and stamping her hoof. Rust rains earthward in gritty showers, along with twigs and primeval muck from the gutter; the roof, corrugated iron set at a lazy slope, creaks and drums with the rampage. On the roof alongside Horsegirl is her wrath, which pounds the iron like a physical thing: Horsegirl and her fury are like two black fighting crows.

"Get lost!" she screams, and whisks her deadly reins. Because the building is high, two stories plus an attic where chairs and files and pageant props are stored, the reins lash nowhere near any child. And because they are so safe where they stand, the children have turned brave. They would never dare heckle her were she on the ground; but she isn't on the ground, and her pride won't let her down to defend herself, so she is at their mercy, of which children have little or none. They buzz below like an excited swarm, like wolves that have spotted the weakling. Horsegirl stares savagely at them, baring her fangs. "I'll jump!" she threatens. "I'm gonna jump!"

"What did she say?"

"She says she'll jump!"

The children move as one, a mass of wasps turning on the wind. Those nearest to the wall step back to give her splattering space. Horsegirl rears away from the edge, her hands moving madly in the air. She throws her head from side to side. Far below they can hear her garbling curses and spells; they hear the moan of the iron as her weight falls on its weak spots. Her burning face juts over the gutter. "I wanna see Mr. Palmer!"

Mr. Palmer is the only teacher for whom Horsegirl has any respect. Three righteous girls have already hotfooted to the staff room with news of the mad girl's latest escapade, and the teachers will arrive at any moment. The children know there's not much time—their excitement tightens like a bolt. The air is suddenly peppery with stones. Someone kicks a soccer ball, and it bounds thickly off the wall. Rubbish is hurled, paper bags and wadded gum and the wrappings of flavored ice blocks. She claws at them, shredding air, beyond the range of even the strongest boy, the most canny aim. The teachers are rushing across the playground when one voice finally yells it, determined not to be deprived. It's a hoarse sound, a myna's cry: *"Jump!"* And there's no persuasion needed for a chorus to rise instantly behind it, fire rushing through grass. "Jump! Jump! *Jump!"*

Horsegirl gazes down at them, her mouth gaping wide. The cresting crowd of innocents laughs, claps, alive. It hoots and whistles with glee. A boy snatches Adrian's bag of Chikadees and crushes filthy fists into the phosphorescent yellow balls. "Jump!" the vandal whoops, crystals of snack flying, bouncing on his toes. *"Jump! Come on!"*

"Jump, whydontcha? *Jump!"*

"Do it, jump—"

The teachers wade amongst them, hurling children aside. A tiny girl is knocked to the ground; another child buckles, clutching at his face. Horsegirl wails, spotting Mr. Palmer. Beyond her, the sky is hoary white and gray. "Mr. Palmer! Mr. Palmer!"

The children run riot while they still have their chance. "Mr. Palmer, Mr. Palmer!" chant the noisiest, while the bullies begin to shove and pinch. The school yard is slashed with shrill cries, blurred by the fragmenting crowd. Several youngsters put their hands over their ears; one or two start to hysterically scream. Other children snatch the opportunity to bellow. "Jump! Jump!"

"Horsehead, horsehead, jump, jump!"

Adrian, on the outskirts, seeks Clinton, who giggles doubtfully, eyes fixed on Horsegirl. He too is yelping, though not loudly, "Jump?"

Adrian looks to the sky, biting his lip. He tastes the false flavor of Chikadees. All the children are glancing at each other, darting dark inspections. Solidarity is important; there's only strength in a crowd. "Jump!" he says, because he cannot be seen to do otherwise. He hopes she won't—he knows he would never see a more horrifying sight than the tumbling of that gangly girl—but he is obligated to encourage her, though the word catches in his chest. "Jump! Jump!"

"Get out of here!" Mr. Palmer shouts it, and a few are shocked into silence. Others push forward, hammering the wall. Mr. Palmer slings them aside like cats. "Get lost, you little bastards!"

"Make them shut up!" Horsegirl is lying along the gutter, one leg flung over the side; the reins and bridle are knotted around her hands. "I'm gonna jump!" she's yelling, "I'm gonna jump!" And Adrian steps back, at that moment convinced that she will. A moldy rain of decay and leaves plummets to the ground.

In that instant the school bell rings. The children spin to confront the sound. The bell monitor, a sturdy girl from Adrian's grade, is striding across the yard, giving hefty swings to the bronze bell. Her face is set like concrete, as flinty as shale. She rings the bell with a terrible authority. The crowd is swiftly muted, though they sense that they've been dudded: children on their lunch break, like lonesome animals on a chain, have a feeling for time. A grumble of mutiny rolls over the asphalt: few of them wear watches, and even fewer can tell the time, but Clinton has a diver's watch, and Paul, standing near, grabs the boy's wrist, brandishing his arm in the air. "There's ten more minutes!" he trumpets. "We've still got ten more minutes!"

"Get out of here!" Mr. Palmer roars. In each hand he's gripping a shirt, shaking the brains from the child inside it. Other teachers are toiling through the crowd, swatting heads and backsides. Horsegirl, flattened against the roof, is howling at the clouds. "Get to your classrooms!" commands the principal. "Nasty little dogs," Adrian hears a teacher say. Clinton is torn from Paul's grip, sucked away by the churn of the crowd. The monitor relentlessly rings the bell; her ears are beginning to hurt. The pack breaks into smaller clumps, splintered by angry adults. Such is the bell's power that even the most unruly thug feels its pull and slouches from the shadow of the wall. There's chuckling and chatter as the children return to their rooms, but they understand that the game is now over.

Adrian, alone at his desk, nicks his thumb until it stings. He knows it was wrong to say the word *jump*—he wishes he could gulp the word from the past and swallow it back down. At the same time, he's glad that some kids saw him say it—glad that, when they are punished, he will be given an equal share. He feels the gnawing of guilt and remorse, but it's a fair price to pay for not singling himself out.

What really worries him is the empty desk in the corner, the craziness that seems sunk into the wood, the fact that no one seems to regret her absence, the recognition of how much they despise her. How much, out there, he too had despised her, and still shamefully does.

His left hand, trembling on the table, hankers for the bronze bowl.

Nicole listens to the story and says, "I wish that she had jumped."

Joely squeezes into a ball at the thought, says, "*Grrr.*"

They are sitting, with toddler Giles, at the base of the liquidambar in Adrian's front yard. The earth is moist and oozy, but they've perched themselves on the tree's thick roots, which writhe like anacondas to the surface and below again. Nicole leans forward, pushing the sole of her sneaker into the soft ground. "What happened next? Did the girl come back to class?"

"Nope."

"How come?" Joely unsqueezes, sitting up. "Where did she go?"

"Maybe she *did* jump," her sister suggests. "Just because you didn't see her—"

"We did see her. One kid was looking out the window. He saw her walking round the playground."

"What do you mean—they just let her walk around? Like a wild animal?"

"Like a wild animal!" Joely crows.

109

Adrian nods vigorously, pleased they understand. "She was digging in the preps' sandpit."

"In the *sandpit*?" Nicole cannot fathom it. "What was she doing in the *sandpit*?"

"She really *is* crazy!" Joely marvels.

Nicole leans against the ambar's fissured trunk. "I reckon she should have jumped. When you say you're going to do something, you should do it."

The evening is rapidly closing, and the air is very still. When a car sweeps silently past on the road, it is a fleet but curious interruption. Giles is gathering dropped leaves and presenting them, one at a time and with great ceremony, to Adrian, who keeps them in his lap. The children sit facing Nicole's house, with its high unwholesome-yellow walls and bristling blue wrought iron. For the first time it occurs to Adrian that the house, Mr. Jeremio's pride and joy, is an eyesore. He has never, before this moment, thought to pass aesthetic judgment on his surroundings. "Remember that lady," Joely murmurs, and both he and Nicole know which woman she is thinking about, for the ruminations of each of them are anchored here, on their houses, on their neighbors, on the junction of the roads. "She was crazy too."

"Maybe she wasn't!"

Nicole speaks so sharply that the three children blink nervously at her, sensing rising danger. The girl's cheeks are wan with cold; her fingertips are rosy. "Maybe she *wasn't* crazy. Maybe that lady was right. Maybe we *aren't* who we say. Maybe my name's not Nicole. How would *you* know?"

With this she jabs a nail into Adrian's side. He pulls away, scattering leaves. Nicole darts closer, yowls, "Who do *you* think I am?"

He doesn't know how to answer—he's never met anyone as frightening as she. His mouth flaps like a fishtail. "I don't know—"

"You don't know *anything*. I'll tell you. I'm *Miss Terious*, that's who." She springs suddenly to her feet and skips like a ballerina through the grass. She frolics in a circle, pirouetting around the tree. The children watch, slack-jawed. The dancing makes her dizzy, and she puffs out clouds of air. She staggers drunkenly to Adrian and flicks him, quick as snakebite, under the chin. It makes his heart jump. "I'll tell you who I am," she pants, bending down to him. *"I'm the girl that everyone's looking for."*

Joely goes beetle-browed, confused. Nicole stands on tiptoe, tilting to the ghostly moon. "I am!" she sings, to someone living on the stars. "No one knows it, but I am! I'm the girl who made them cry! I've lost my mum, I've lost my dad, and everyone's looking for me!"

She glares at the children, who stare, amazed, at her. "Ha!" she barks, brisk as a terrier—then she's off and running, hair flying like a pirate's flag, her long legs kicking the hem of her dress. She sprints over the road and charges along the street, and when their view is blocked by fences, they still hear, for a minute, the slap of her soles on concrete. Giles's eyebrows creep together; he tugs thoughtfully on an ear. Adrian looks at Joely. "That's not true, is it?" he says. "You're not lost, are you?"

"No!" The idea makes her laugh delightedly, when her house is just over the road. "Nicole's crazy like that girl at your school!"

Adrian feels foolish and relieved. Joely stands up, shaking specks of grass from her skirt. She's wearing woolen tights that make green twigs of her legs. She says, "My mum wants to see you."

"What?" He feels the blood pool in his cheeks. "Why? I haven't done anything—"

"Mmph, she just wants to meet you. You're not in any trouble."

Giles upturns his palm so his sister may take his

hand. Adrian wavers. "It's nearly teatime. Gran might get cross."

Joely nods and shrugs. "OK." Adrian is stabbed with desperation: no one's mother has ever asked to meet him before. He finds his feet, brushing his damp haunches. "Maybe if I'm quick," he says.

He has been inside their house in the days before anybody lived there—he's been inside when it wasn't even a house, just an arrangement of timber cluttering the sky. He had been young then, for the house had taken years to build—when Mr. Jeremio poured the gray foundations, Adrian was a little kid. He was older when the staircase took shape beneath the carpenter's hands, the banister rail carved from a single length of teak. His mother would bring him to visit his gran, and, after picking a flat tune out of the piano and reexamining the drawerful of matchboxes from all over the world, the idle boy had invariably found himself wandering over the road. Mr. Jeremio had let him explore as he pleased, providing he kept out of the way. He liked Mr. Jeremio's reasons for renting out the big house and keeping the small one as his own: "I don't want to take up much space on this earth." He knows the house as if he's lived in it: he knows the rooms; he knows the views. He mostly knows what he's going to see even before he steps through the door.

They do not have much furniture. There is a thick, porridgy smell. There are a couple of dirty foot marks on the beige carpet in the hall. The important noise of a television travels down the stairs. Pictures lean against walls, waiting to be hung. Joely leaves Giles to totter alone, beckons Adrian with a curled finger. The master bedroom is on the ground floor—Adrian has always been impressed by the fact that it sprouts its own bathroom. He has expected to meet the mother in the living room or the kitchen, but Joely pushes aside the bedroom door.

The room is pink, the wallpaper flocked—it's like being inside a rosebud. The first thing he sees is a high expanse of bed, topped and tailed with carved bedsteads, plush with blankets the color of powder. The lady lying below these blanched covers is something he almost fails to see. Across his mind flits the image of his grandfather, dying beneath the quilts. "Mum," says Joely, "this is Adrian."

He hangs back, frozen by the knowledge of sickness in the room. Joely has gone to the side of the bed, close to where her mother is propped on pillows. On the wall around the bed head are splashes of color on crinkled paper, paintings done by the girls. On a bedside table is a photograph of the children. The mother's voice is like a bird's wing brushing glass. "Adrian," she whispers, "it's nice to meet you."

He shuffles closer, and her eyes follow him. "Hello," he mumbles: he doesn't know what's wrong with her and isn't sure what to say. He stops where her ankles must be, unwilling to go nearer. Glancing up fleetly, he sees how boneless she is, how she lacks a living thing's quick energy. Her lips are silver and peeling. She wears a floral nightdress and, round her shoulders, a fussy crocheted shawl. Her fingernails have been lacquered sun red, as if she hasn't forgotten happier things.

Her voice is slow, a record playing at wrong speed. "What's the day like, Adrian?"

"It's cold." He hesitates before resting his hands on the blankets, a gesture he hopes seems friendly. *Cold* is unimaginative, and he wonders what she would prefer to hear, this lady who can't leave the room. "The birds are hiding," he says.

Her eyes go crescent. "Poor things. Which is your favorite?"

He thinks. "I like the black-and-white ones."

"Magpies?"

"No, smaller—"

"Larks?"

He nods. "Larks."

"I like larks too." She smiles at him, and Adrian smiles.

"Do you want a drink, Mum?" Joely asks her.

There's something tender and private about the little girl holding a plastic mug to the lips of her mother, and Adrian looks away. The curtains have been drawn across the window, so recently that they sway. In one corner stands a metal trolley designed to slide neatly above the bed. On its tray are a bowl and a coffee cup. Tucked into the gap between the wardrobe and wall is a folded-up wheelchair. It has an unused, retiring look.

Joely dabs dry her mother's chin. The woman coughs and says, "Excuse me."

Her feet, snowed in under the blankets, make only the slightest bulge. Her hands are white and fragile as flour. Although she is not gaunt, she hardly dents her pillow. "I'm told you live with your grandmother, Adrian."

"Yes." He wishes she wouldn't speak; every word sounds scoured out of her. She smiles again, and even that must hurt.

"How lucky you are. I would have loved to live with my grandmama, when I was a little girl."

He nods again, at the carpet. The room is so quiet that he hears the blankets sigh. He feels the woman's hazel consideration of every inch of him; then she takes pity and looks away. "You'd better get home for dinner," she suggests. "Your grandmother will be worried."

He nods, his head loose on his neck. "It was nice meeting you," he says, and he means it, though he never wants to return. Part of him understands why Nicole would claim to have lost her mother; another part thinks that, were this lady his own mother, he could never bear to leave her side.

Once outdoors, in gloomy light, he breathes as deep as he can. He runs up the sloping driveway, feeling the magic workings of his muscles and bones. He arrives late for tea, and Gran is displeased. To punish his tardiness, she won't discuss ailing neighbors with him. Exasperated, she says, "Tell me why you have to know everything?"

Aunt Marta comes for dinner that night. Adrian is, as usual, made unwelcome at the dining table. He sits in the living room, on the overstuffed couch. The couch's hide is golden velvet, and sitting on it makes him feel like a prince. He thinks back on his strange day—of Horse-girl on the iron roof and pawing through the sand, of

Nicole dancing around the liquidambar, of her mother's gauzy voice in the room. He feels as though he lives between sheets of glass, unable to touch the things that happen around him. Everyone and everything exists in a world he cannot quite comprehend. He glimpses only the residue, scrapes the surface of happenings. He wonders if, when he's older, he will better understand things, or if he is doomed to live forever as someone struggling to see.

But he can't relax or get comfortable, wary of grime jumping from himself to the pristine couch. He has come here to touch the holy relic, the cherub bowl, but his eyes are drawn along the mantelshelf to the lanky porcelain figurine that stands at the far end regarding the bowl disdainfully, a saluki peering down at a toad. The figure's name is Royal Doulton, which means she's a princess or queen, and she has patronizing ways. She carries a closed parasol like a rifle on her shoulder. The bowl squats, scowling; the willowy porcelain lady knows her own loveliness and flaunts it, her sultry face, her glossy glaze, her delicacy of build. Adrian slips off the couch and goes to her. Maybe Nicole's mother had looked like this lady; maybe Gran once had. Perplexingly, Royal Doulton looks a little bit like Horsegirl.

As soon as he lifts her off the mantel, she slithers like an eel from his hands. There's something sly and traitorous in the way she shatters to pieces on the bricks of the hearth. There is a shriek behind him—a bloodcurdling scream, really. He hears cutlery dropped and the glass door flung back, and as he feels his grandmother bearing down like a train he crosses himself superstitiously, awaiting the sting of the slap.

She's still furious the next morning, and Adrian can't find his school shoe. He has hobbled about all morning, searching frantically. When Gran's reversing the tank down the drive, Adrian is underneath his bed, scouting the dustiest shadows. The first time she blares the horn, a squeak of dismay escapes him. The second time, frustrated tears fill his eyes. He runs lopsidedly to the den, although he's already looked there. His grandmother leans on the horn as he crouches on the carpet, cheeks scorching, unable to think. He faces the prospect of wearing his sneakers—perhaps his *slippers*—to school, when anything but black lace-ups is strictly forbidden. A salty tear slinks past his nose, and he wretchedly smears it away. Suddenly, salvation: he remembers reading *National Geographic* in bed and, growing sleepy, dropping the magazine to the floor.

He charges to his room, kicks *Geographic* aside, and there it is, the prodigal shoe.

In the car, driving to school, his grandmother doesn't say anything, except to curse the traffic. Adrian cowers like a dog that's been thoroughly thrashed. When he finally dares to glance at her, he sees she's grown fins and horns, fangs and claws.

Things surely cannot get any worse, but that evening they do. His homework demands the use of black ink, so he goes to Rory's bedroom to dig out a pen. He doesn't like Rory's bleak, odoriferous room, nor is he particularly welcome within it, so he hurries, eager to be out. Rory's easel stands empty, so there's no reason for Adrian to think the spats of wayward paint on it should be wet—but some of them must be, for as he ducks by the easel, a dab of British racing green touches the elbow of his sweater. He stares at the spot in abject horror. His grandma nags him to change out of his uniform when he gets home from school, but Adrian is lazy and always reluctant to swap warm clothes for cold, so he disregards this decree when he can. Now there's green paint on his school sweater and the sweater is new, not even one year old: his grandmother, already angry about Royal Doulton and the shoe, will certainly murder him.

He rummages through Rory's painting stuff for a rag, dousing it with turpentine. He rubs the rag determinedly on the stain, and the wool of the sweater darkens and frays. The small green splat spreads to become a noticeably large teal smudge. Adrian gulps down air, mortified. He scuttles to the bathroom, hooking the latch through the eye. He wriggles from the sweater, which reeks of turpentine. He holds the sleeve under the hot tap, gouging soap through the wool. The soap foams and water spits, and the sweater's sleeve is soaked: still the stain remains. The hot water burns him; the soap's smell of flowers rises in the air. Adrian flops on a chair, weak with defeat and melancholy. "You dumb kid," Rory will chortle later; the boy's grandmother will be less amused. To her, who grew up poor, the ruining of good clothes is tenfold more disgraceful than the manslaughter of a china girl: even though he doesn't try, Gran says, "Don't talk to me, Adrian, don't say a word!"

That night he sleeps with his hands clamped between his knees, waking abruptly several times. He wonders what will become of him, a useless, hopeless boy.

On the way to school the following morning, he tentatively speaks up. "Can I stay the night at Clinton's on the weekend, Gran?"

She skewers him in the rearview mirror. "Has Mrs. Tull invited you?"

". . . No."

"Then I don't suppose you can, if you haven't been invited."

He looks out the window, his eyelids fluttering. His sweater smells of turpentine and lavender, and the sleeve isn't thoroughly dry. Paint still marks the elbow like a broad grass stain. As the car pulls up outside the school, he murmurs, "If I ask and his mum says yes, then can I go?"

She eyes him severely, sunlight slanting on her glasses. "I suppose so," she sighs, and spares him a miserly smile. "Have a good day."

The tank heaves away from the gutter, and Beattie looks in the mirror to see him standing where she'd left him, his hair a mess, children bustling past him, the straps of the satchel tangled round his fingers. She has an urge to stop, run back, straighten his uniform, tidy his hair, tweak some color into his cheeks, but he'll never learn discipline if she babies him, so she drives resolutely on.

As soon as they've wished her good morning, before they've even sat down, the substitute teacher tells them that Sandra won't be returning to class. The children look blank—they don't immediately equate Horsegirl with the demureness of Sandra. She's been absent from the classroom since the incident on the rooftop, a day and a half ago. Her classmates have assumed she's resting, letting her battiness subside; now they realize she isn't going to return, that her desk will stay empty forever. "What's gonna happen to her?" one child, bolder than the rest, their ambassador, demands to be told.

"Sandra's going to a special place. A place that can care for children like her."

"Crazy kids, you mean?"

Someone might have dropped an ice block down her dress, for the teacher jolts a bit. "No, *not* crazy kids. It's unkind to call people names. Sandra is your friend. She has some problems, but that's all right. All of us have problems now and then, don't we?"

The children mutter, refusing to commit. None will admit to having problems if problems lead to rooftops and assorted special places. "Sandra's going somewhere they can take proper care of her," says the teacher, and to her mind the pupils accept the explanation and sit down in cheerful readiness to begin their day. But Adrian is not the only child who is fervently praying *Please don't let me be like that please don't let me be crazy I am not the same*

123

as her I'm wanted someone wants me I don't belong to St. Jonah's—

The moment he can he asks Clinton if he might stay Saturday night at his friend's house. Clinton is easygoing; he doesn't need his mother's permission for anything. "Yeah," he says. "Bring the Slinky."

See, thinks Adrian, *see?*

The newspaper carries an item in a corner of a page, no more than two or three paragraphs long. It's a story that is perhaps too poignant to be mentioned on TV. A witness to the vanishing of the Metfords has been taken to hospital to have her stomach pumped. This is the housewife who was second to see the children on their journey to the shop, the woman shaking crumbs from a mat. The woman's husband says his wife keeps seeing the children as she saw them, so briefly, two and a half weeks ago. Veronica holds Christopher's hand; young Zoe dawdles behind: after them strides the Thin Man, silent as a fox. The husband says his wife will probably never forgive herself for letting them just walk on.

Seven

He loves Clinton's house, cluttered as it is like a Christmas tree, where the heating and the television are always turned up high. Clinton's mother is massive and prone to hollering, occasionally at her kids and her husband, but mostly at everything else in the world, which irritates her to no end. It is always easiest to do what she wants, to believe whatever she says. Her husband never does anything without first asking her if it's right that he do so; he exists in his house unobtrusively, a tiny spider sharing the web of a giant. She adores her two children in a heavy-handed way and informs others of how magnificent they are; in her opinion they're cut from angelic cloth, and her days revolve around them; she seems to float without purpose, like a gaudy balloon, when they step out from her expansive shadow. Now that both Clinton and his sister are at school, she lurks around the staff room, volunteers for snack shop and library duty, supervises excursions. Adrian sees that she doesn't realize how her presence embarrasses her son.

She likes Adrian because he is so harmless: it's beyond the boy's capabilities to lead Clinton astray.

The house is filled to bursting point with plates and ornaments and china-faced dolls, with commemorative statues and porcelain creatures and silk flowers under bell jars, with the great hordes of tackiness that are advertised in women's magazines and that Mrs. Tull is unable to resist. Every second day another parcel arrives; every other day she's writing a check. Glass cabinets make insecure cages for herds of cavorting unicorns and Baby Animals of the World; on a high shelf in the hallway mope doll-sized replicas of Marilyn, Buddy, JFK, and James Dean, members of the incomplete collection of Those Taken Before Their Time. A genuine Swiss cuckoo clock regularly strangles the living-room air; talk radio dominates the kitchen, and an irate dachshund pretends to doze on the sunroom couch. On the weekend Mrs. Tull lets her children eat Froot Loops for lunch. Clinton has never been smacked in his life, and the whole family gathers to nitpick their way through their favorite TV shows. Once the dachshund had bitten Adrian, and Mr. Tull had encouraged the boy to bite the dog right back. He'd been disappointed when Adrian refused.

His gran drops him off soon after lunch and waits, engine thrumming, until Mrs. Tull has opened the front door. Privately, Mrs. Tull thinks Beattie has a face like a thunderclap; Beattie has her own opinion of Mrs. Tull, including the prognosis that the woman will be deservedly dead from a heart attack before she's forty years old. Face to face, the ladies are impeccably polite.

"Clinton's in the garage, honey." Adrian likes the way she takes his coat and bag from him, as if he's someone important. He tells her that Beattie has sent over a packet of Tic-Tocs, and Mrs. Tull forages for them in the bag. Every one of the cookies will be gone before sunset, and Mr. Tull will complain of a gooby stomach.

He knows the house well; it is friendly to him. He likes the multitude of mail-order goods—he likes the plate that, wound on its base, tinkles the tune of "Silent Night"; he likes the thimbles shaped like woodland animals. Throughout the house the television competes noisily with the radio; in the hallway he's blown sideways by the heater's parching gale. He slips through the back door and trots down the path to the garage. Clinton comes out of the darkness, shading his eyes from the white sky. His glasses and his shoes are coated in a fine smoky dust. He asks, "Did you bring the Slinky?"

"It's in my bag, inside. Will I get it?"

"No, later. We're breaking things."

Adrian blinks. His friend is not typically destructive: he has much, so he wastes things and loses things, but he doesn't usually ruin them. "What are we breaking?"

Clinton turns on his heels. "Not *you*," he says. "You only just got here."

Adrian slopes after him, into the garage. Neither Mr. nor Mrs. Tull likes to throw much away, and their garage, like their house, is a repository for the many things they will never need. There's no light bulb, and daylight angles only with difficulty past the barnlike doors. At first, Adrian sees just murk. Then his eyes find their way through the pitch, and he sees, heaped in corners, the hundreds of boxes that brought the mail-order goods to their new owner unscathed. The boxes leak plastic and screwed-up balls of paper. His gaze climbs down them to the floor, where the remains of a wooden chest of drawers lie splayed on the concrete. Ugly and cheaply made, the drawers have been banished out here long enough to be laced with web and specked with mildew. Now they're wreckage, a broken-backed jumble of timber and nails, remorselessly smashed to pieces. Adrian, staring down at it, sees a worried daddy long legs fumbling in search of a safer home. "How did you do it?" he asks, for he would have had no clue where to begin.

"With this." Clinton hefts a baseball bat not much shorter than himself.

Adrian crouches, touching a finger to the tips of a wrenched staple. The way the chest of drawers lies there, its frame flattened, disemboweled, it's clear its death was torture. The cavernous quiet of the garage makes Adrian's ears ring; the dimness is a strain to see through. "Why did you do it?" he wonders, for it seems so wanton, so unlike anything Clinton's ever done.

"For fun," his friend says blithely. "It was *fun*." He glares through the glass, which enlarges and liquefies his eyes, challenging Adrian to dispute the claim—wanting and daring and *encouraging* Adrian to dispute it, so his churlishness may take flight. And Adrian shuffles warily, for Clinton is not usually like this. "I've got a surprise for you," his friend informs him.

". . . What?"

Clinton smirks and slings the bat into a city of boxes.

The impact sends beach chairs, paint tins, plant pots tumbling down. From the midst of the crashing cascade jumps a spritelike, triumphant boy. With the noise and swirling dust and the darkness, it takes Adrian a moment to recognize Paul. "Hi," he mutters, affable enough despite his shock, despite the fact that he's queasy inside, despite feeling like he could cry. Clinton has thrown his head back and is laughing raucously, spine arched, cackling, the sound scraping off the iron roof. Paul pounces through the remnants of the chest of drawers, kicking the fragments across the floor. "You should see what we've got planned for the Slinky!" he bays.

Adrian bridles, shaking his head. "What? What are you gonna do?"

Paul props a foot on the drawers. "Let's just say," he says coolly, "it won't be doing much slinking anymore."

Adrian looks at Clinton, whose grinning face falls a little. "It's only a stupid toy," the boy says, sullenly.

Adrian looks back at Paul, his heart sinking to his shoes. Paul is tall and fast on his feet; he is the cleverest boy in the class and the best swimmer in the school: once, on holiday at the beach, he'd rescued a floundering child from the waves. He is aristocratically choosy about his acquaintances and could have befriended any kid in the class, maybe anyone in the entire school: he didn't need Clinton. But Adrian has no one except Clinton, and he can't share. He can't compete with Paul, who is louder, stronger, smarter, funnier, who has such credentials, who is so enviable. There's no reason why Clinton should keep Adrian as a comrade, now that he has this glittering alternative—Adrian sees that his friend brims with glee-fulness at being chosen by this high-status boy. Adrian is overthrown, and Paul knows it: he stands amid the splinters of destruction and grins, baring teeth like tomb-stones. The two boys gaze at each other, and Adrian wants to ask the usurper why he's done this thing—why pick on *him*, such poor competition—he'd like to know why he's worthy of such an act of malignance. Maybe Paul wants access to Clinton's resources; maybe he's done this simply because he can. "Go get the Slinky now," says Clinton.

"Yeah," snaps Paul, "hurry."

He realizes what they'll do to the toy, understands that as soon as they get their hands on it, it will become rubbish. But he has not the will to resist them—some-times sacrifices must be made. If he lets them take some-thing precious from him, they might let him remain their friend. Maybe they will let him sit inconspicuous on the edge. This is what he tells himself, as if jollying along someone much less knowing than he. As he trudges to the house, he knows it's not going to happen this way: he knows he is as routed as the chest of drawers on the garage floor.

After Adrian's father had done what the authorities told him to do and taken Adrian from his mother, Adrian had continued to attend the same school he had always gone to, despite now living farther away. He had walked to school and home again while he lived with Sookie; after moving in with his father, he'd become a passenger on the school's tubby bus. Everyone—his father, his father's girl-friend, his father's parents, who lived in another coun-try—said it was a good thing, Adrian staying at his old school: if his home life must be disrupted, at least his education would feel no hitch, and nor would he know the stress of having to make new friends.

Then, as now, Adrian only wanted one companion. Tow-headed Damien was generally good-natured, but he had a venomous streak. One afternoon in art class, he had grabbed Adrian's wrist, sending the paintbrush careering. "Whoops," he laughed, "you must be drunk!" He had shaken the brush from Adrian's grip and hit Adrian in the mouth with the boy's own knuckles. "You must be drunk, you must be drunk!" Damien cawed again and again, while Adrian struggled to avoid the hard cuffing of his hand. His classmates giggled and shouted, quick to take up the cry. "He must be drunk! Adrian's drunk!"

The teacher had yanked the ringleader by the scruff, smacking a ruler on his calves. Damien yelled like a bull. The other children snuffled and snorted, shutting up fast. The diversion passed, the ruler welts vanished, but black bruises had been raised: both Adrian and Damien understood that their friendship was done.

A child often lacks the experience to see immediately what he's lost. It took a few days before it dawned on Adrian that school is a lonely ordeal for the child who lacks company. He wasn't a gregarious boy, he couldn't push his way into any existing group of friends; he felt that, having nothing to offer, they would recognize him as a parasite and treat him with contempt. The reason he felt he had nothing to offer was that, in his heart, he knew he was dull. Nothing about him gave him value: he was ordinary and dull. But at least he was smart enough to know it: he wouldn't be one of those wretches who lurk the perimeters, who live the hideous role of whipping boy, lackey, buffoon. He exiled himself ruthlessly, which at least was dignified. He could not be injured if he shielded himself from harm.

But school is a terrible place for a rejected child. The ringing of the lunchtime bell was enough to cool his blood; the lunch hour seemed an endless desert of time. He didn't complain or resist going to school, but every day he haunted the gates, hoping against hope that his mother would walk by, discover him, and carry him away. She didn't, but eventually he went anyway. When his grandmother told him he would attend a different school while living with her, he knew she was surprised that he wasn't a bit perturbed. It is, after all, common knowledge that normal children are upset to leave their friends.

Adrian has never thought that what happened to him had been cruel—children inhabit an animalistic world and accept with grace its harsh rules. He never considered anyone to blame but himself, really. But he'd been glad of the gift of anonymity that the new school gave him: at just eight years of age, he had started over again.

Now, still only nine, he must begin again. Today is Saturday: Monday waits like an ax.

Eventually he gathers his courage and, breaking one of Gran's commandments, asks Mrs. Tull if he might use the phone. She does not seem to greet the request as the outrage Gran assures him it is: she says, "You can call anyone you like, sweetie, as long as you don't call me late for breakfast." The dial is heavy to turn, slow to rotate back to place. *Land of the Giants* is on telly, midgets in flight from heads the size of mountains. The dachshund stares uncivilly from the couch, its body a readied missile. The tone *brr*s four times before Rory answers it.

Adrian is aware of Mrs. Tull listening, though she's looking at the TV. He tries to keep his voice low, beneath the midget wailing. "Is Gran there, Uncle?"

"No, she's out. What's the matter?"

He twines the cord around his fingers. "Will she be home soon, do you know?"

His uncle sounds doubtful. "She's shopping. That takes hours. What's the matter?" he asks again.

Adrian searches for a way of saying it. He doesn't want to offend Mrs. Tull. "I don't feel well," he whispers. "I want to come home."

There's silence at the end of the line. Then Rory says, "What's happened, Adrian?"

"Nothing," the boy answers. "I just want to come home."

Once more, Rory pauses. Adrian hears the dog

135

scratch its sleek hide. His fingers are trapped in the clutches of the cord. He longs for the protection of his home, his bedroom; he would give anything to be rescued from here. His heart is drenched in a paining grief. Uncle and nephew listen to each other's breathing, and both of them are thinking, *There is no use to me.*

"When Beattie comes home, I'll tell her to come and get you."

". . . OK."

"Maybe she won't be long, Adrian."

"OK. I've got to go."

"I'll see you soon, all right?"

"Yes." Adrian's voice is hollow. "I have to go."

He hangs up; from the corner of an eye, he sees Mrs. Tull studying him. "You feeling sick?" she asks.

He nods faintly. "Gran's coming to get me."

She looks at him—looks *into* him—and it shocks him to realize she knows very well what's happened in the garage; also that she will never fault Clinton, never lay any blame on her son. She looks embedded in the recliner, her eyes like seeds fallen on the vast facial terrain. She has a muckraker's reputation, and it occurs to Adrian that she's probably uncovered every secret thing about him—about his mother and father, about his pariah past. It's likely that she knows he walks the very brink of belonging to St. Jonah's.

Maybe she's told Clinton this, and maybe Clinton has forsaken him because it's best to dissociate oneself from some things. Maybe, at school on Monday, his ex-friend means to spread these shaming truths he has learned. The class won't have time to miss Horsegirl.

"Tic-Toc?" Mrs. Tull offers him the ravaged pack; Adrian shakes his head, hedging for the door. Outside, the Slinky lies in a tangled snarl, its quicksilver perfection destroyed. Adrian goes back out to the yard, to wait, to smile, to laugh, pretend.

Rory is lying in bed reading when he hears the small noise, a sound like the private mutterings of some tiny creature. He lowers the book, listening. In a moment, when the noise does not stop, he gets out of bed, his head cocked like a dog's.

In the hushed hallway the sound is louder. The venetian blinds have not been lowered, and moonlight lacquers the polished floor. Beattie has long gone to bed; Rory hears the click of the hallway clock, loud in the empty air. He steps quietly on lean bare feet, the cord of his robe flicking his knees. He nudges Adrian's bedroom door, and the hinges groan; the mystery sound is instantly stilled, and Rory says, "Adrian?"

The boy's voice is crushed. *"Mmh?"*

"What's the matter? Why are you crying?"

He hears the child swallow air. "I'm not."

Rory pulls his robe closer, feeling through its toweling and the flannel of his pajamas the night's icy cold. He probes his way across the shadowed floor to switch on the bedside lamp. He crouches by the bed while Adrian blinks and wipes his eyes. The pillowcase has been used to mop tears.

"Tell me what's wrong, Adrian."

". . . Nothing is."

"Was Clinton nasty to you?"

The boy's chest rises painfully. In the stark light of the lamp bulb, his eyes have a sore, burned cast. "No."

"What, then?"

He sets his jaw. "Nothing."

Rory eases the weight off his toes. He wishes he could comfort the child, fight his wars for him, grind to oblivion whatever tragedy has occurred. Instead, he leaves the room. In a minute he returns, carrying with care a large canvas stretched on a frame. The boy has wiped his face with his knuckles; his cheeks look blotchy and swollen.

Rory leans the picture against the legs of a chair, saying, "This is for you."

Adrian sits up on an elbow, shading aside the halo of light. His tender eyes roam the painting. A fanciful, colorful, serpentlike beast is carving through swirling blue waves, white foam spuming in its frothy green wake. In the sky above, a yellow sun shines; the beast's whiskered face wears a cunning, waggish grin. Adrian looks at his uncle. "It's the sea monster."

Rory nods. "Now it's yours. It doesn't matter if it's not on TV. It lives in your bedroom."

The boy smiles; his lashes brush tears on his cheeks. "Thank you."

"The paint's not dry, so be careful. You'll get bitten if you go too close."

Again, Adrian makes a weary effort to smile. Rory stands the painting safely by a wall. He turns to his nephew, rubbing his hands against the cold. The child, crowned by light, dries his face with a sheet. "Feeling better now?"

"Yes." The boy nods adamantly, glancing away.

"Don't forget to turn off the light." Rory moves to the door. "You're really not going to tell me what's wrong?"

Adrian bites his lip. He looks down at the ripples of

blanket, hesitating. In a dull wispy voice he says, "Everybody leaves me. I'm not allowed to be anywhere."

Rory feels the door handle, cool beneath his fingers. He'd thought it would be something much worse, something he could not fix. "Not everyone, Adrian. I won't leave you. You can always stay with me, as long as you want. All right?"

The child's chin wobbles, he stares fiercely at the bedclothes.

"No matter what. I promise. All right?"

The boy nods slackly. "All right."

Rory lingers. When he looks at Adrian, Rory sees the assailed and sensitive child he himself once was. He wants to tell his nephew that it's stupid to be that way, so easily hurt: it's better to be like a plank of wood, an emotional mule. It's best not to feel, he wants to say; best to have the nerve endings cauterized. He says, "Don't forget the lamp."

"I won't."

"See you in the morning, then."

Adrian's eyes dart to him and away, but he's not going to cry now. "Good night," he says, drawing up the blankets. "Thank you for the sea monster."

Midnight means they have been missing for three weeks. In those three weeks, there's been rain. The weather has been chill. The mornings have been misted by fog and diamonded with dew. Some afternoons there's been a breeze that drills straight through to bone. Occasionally there's been watery sunshine, cream colored, pasty, but mostly the days have been cold. It is sad to think of children being out in such weather, and there's a stirring of strange grievance at the knowledge that they haven't been given a warm place to lie.

Eight

A man who says he is psychic claims to know where the Metfords are. This man has had minor success as a visionary in the past, so the police, lacking any serious leads, were prepared to hear him out. Needless to say, they did not want word of this willingness to get around—they didn't want the public realizing the depths of their desperation. Despite their efforts, however, the story has leaked, escaped and flown around twittering like a canary from a cage. This latest development in the case is relayed by television, by newspaper, by stern radio.

"Did you hear what that man reckons?" Nicole is swinging on the garden gate, a thing that would break Mr. Jeremio's heart to see. "He reckons those kids are near water."

"In water, or near it?"

"Near it, he said."

Adrian snorts dismissively. "Everyone's near water."

The gate lurches Nicole back and forth, shuddering when it reaches the extent of its swing and sailing through the arc again. Her cheeks have gone pink with the streaming air. "Why did you visit my mother?" she asks.

Adrian is walking on the top of the fence, one foot on either side of the ribbon of wrought iron. The fence is not a wide one, and his balance teeters. "Joely invited me."

"Joely's only six," Nicole retorts acidly. "What she says doesn't count."

Adrian closes his eyes, rises on tiptoe, shakily holds out his arms. Wind silky as a cat's coat rubs delicately by him. He's free, except for the tips of his toes on the bricks. He asks, "How long has your mum been sick?"

The gate squeals and clangs; he hears the air jolt out of her. "A bit before I was born. A bit more after Joely was born. A lot more after Giles was born."

Adrian's eyes flutter open. "That's a long time."

Nicole's face clouds. She is bowed over the top of the gate, holding on tight with her hands. "Don't talk about her," she warns. "She's not *your* mother, you know."

"I know—"

"She shouldn't be anyone's mother, if all she does is lie in bed all day and die."

Adrian gapes, horrified. "It's mean to say that about your mother."

"How would you know?" Nicole fixes angry eyes on him. "Well, Adrian?"

Gran has reversed the car nearly to the footpath, and he jumps with relief from the fence. "I've got to go."

She doesn't care, continuing to sweep to and fro. Her long jet hair is blown, by the backdraft, across her face.

When he's halfway to the car, she calls his name, and he stops to look around. She's moved from the gate to the garden tap and turned the faucet on hard. Water gushes like a solid crystal stake into the gridded drain, and she shouts above the noise of this suburban cascade. "I'm near water!" she cries out to him. "Near water, see?"

Every Sunday he and his grandmother go to the late-morning Mass. Beattie takes church as if it were medicine: stoically, without humor. Adrian gets so bored his teeth hurt. He wears his second-best outfit, so he's highly uncomfortable. The church is heated as warm as a grave.

If he were more sure of his abilities, he could be an altar boy. Many of the boys in his grade are altar boys and for their efforts get a few coins' reward. But Adrian is certain he'd forget when to ring the bells, would make a mistake and immediately die, so he's condemned to sit beside his gran, stifled by the incense and the droning dreariness. Each week he studies whichever stained glass window looms above their pew—each week his artist's eye is quick to spot the flaws. Peter's head is too big for his body, the dove has the neck of a swan. Everywhere is Jesus trudging out his last few days.

Beattie understands that Rory is unable to leave the house, but she wishes he could make an exception for a weekly visit to church. She worries about him desperately, his body and underfed soul. He is only a young man, just twenty-five: she wonders how he will survive the many years of his future, how long he must exist contained. Some Sundays she cannot shake the aching thought of him from her head; other Sundays he'll beg a prayer from her and she'll refuse to give him one, leaving out his name deliberately, his presumptuousness making her seethe. On these days she swears that if he won't make the effort to help himself, he will get no prayers from her.

Afterward Adrian goes to the corner where he and Clinton often meet to wait patiently while there's chatter among the sin-scrubbed parishioners, and a courtly but vicious joust is fought between the holy and the gentrified that determines who, that week, will monopolize the priest. But Clinton isn't standing in their usual place, as Adrian has expected he won't be.

Once, Adrian and Rory had watched a movie where an escaped convict, charging helter-skelter through jungled land, had tripped a string that launched a raft of spikes up from the ground. The convict had plunged straight into these spikes, skewering himself from head to toe. Adrian feels as if he's run into just such a trap; he remembers the pinioned convict had gurgled, shuddered, and died.

On Monday morning he refuses to go to school. "You're not sick," Beattie tells him. "You were playing on the road all day yesterday, you can't be too sick. Get dressed, Adrian."

But he clamps his mouth and simply looks at her, his gray eyes large in a small, ashy face. He sits in his pajamas on the end of his bed, aimlessly kicking his heels. By now he should be showered and eating breakfast, and time is getting away. "Do you want a belting?" she asks.

He considers this. "If I don't have to go to school."

Beattie hisses air past her teeth, throwing his shirt to the floor. She should make good her threat and smack him, but the truth is she's nonplussed. He has never refused to go to school before—he takes school the way she takes church, with never so much as a whimper. He knows that attendance is one of her rules and that her rules are well nigh set in stone. He must have his reasons for resisting now, when never before. He slouches like an untidy elf, the living image of all that's stubborn. There must be something grim about today, something he's not telling. "Do you have a test?"

"No."

She peers at him, sees he's not lying. "Your teacher's back from her honeymoon today. Don't you want to see her?"

He pauses, not wanting to be unkind. "I'll see her another day."

Grandmother and grandson gaze at each other; her eyes are like beams, unchallengeable, and he glances away defeated. His hands fidget like flies on his knees. "Get dressed, Adrian," Beattie sighs. "I'm tired of this."

She strides for the door. "Please don't make me," he groans.

She marches down the hall and into the kitchen, slamming herself into a chair. His cereal sits waiting, dry as slate in its bowl. His cup of tea stands beside hers, a skin of coolness on the surface of both. There'd been panic and despair in his voice when he asked her *please*.

She sips her tea, the skin breaking into minute continents. She thinks that she's too old for all this: *I've forgotten what I'm meant to do.*

Capitulation now will certainly mark the beginning of an unstoppable erosion—soon enough he'll be disobeying every one of her commands *(soon he'll be a teenager, run completely wild)*. Yet Beattie feels an inexplicable desire to let him do as he wants: she has the peculiar sensation that, should she send him off to school, some dreadful harm will come to him.

She puts her cup down with a splash and marches along the hall to his room. He is standing beside the bed, slipping thin arms into a school shirt. It pleases her to see he's succumbed to authority and is doing what he's told, but her mind, finally made up, won't now be changed.

"If you stay home," she growls, "you have to stay in bed. No television, nothing. If you're sick, you rest. I don't want to see your face or hear your voice. And don't you smile at me."

She spins on her feet, slams the door after her. *I'm too old for this,* she insists to herself, and yet she does feel better.

He lies in bed for hours, flipping through the pages of *National Geographic.* He glances now and then at his Batman clock and wonders what's happening at school. The teacher, returned from her honeymoon, would be in a good mood. She'd be glad to see them, want to know what work they'd done. She would ask what had happened to Horse-girl, and a serious girl would recount the misadventures; there'd be additional asides offered from those who perceived she was forgetting important details. Their teacher would listen, and then she would explain the disappearance to them in a way that made it seem less menacing.

His back gets sore and he wriggles around. Rory visits and they play Battleship. In the afternoon he surprises himself by falling into thick, claggy sleep. When he wakes, the blankets are knotted round his stomach and his head vaguely hurts. He stares in a daze at the sea monster, at its dapples of glittery gold. He's made a mistake by staying home, he sees that now, but it is too late to change.

On Tuesday morning he gets dressed for school without a word of protest. He keeps his distance from Clinton in class. At recess he doesn't go to the usual place beside the drinking fountains outside the restrooms: instead he takes his snack, two biscuits wedged with butter and jam, down to the school gates. He hoists himself to the top of the wall and sits so his legs dangle free, so part of him, at least, is not fenced in.

It had been a mistake staying home yesterday because his absence had whispered surrender. From his eyrie on the wall, Adrian sees Paul do a crazy jig, a victory dance solely for him. He looks away, nibbling the biscuits. He decides to stop regretting his missed day of school—it might have appeared a tactical error, but it wasn't really. His presence would not have kept Clinton loyal; it wouldn't have fended off Paul. He chooses to see his peaceful day at home as one hard day he had not spent at school.

Inside himself he's crawling, though, flailing in quicksands of anguish. He does not know what he's going to do.

He shifts on his perch, watching the cars on the road. A ghost of himself is proud that he sits, head up, with dignity. No one watching would guess how he feels. There are years of this life ahead of him. Just one year is a long time, unfathomable. His lips move silently as he counts the cars passing, for want of something to do.

It's the going-home bell he looks forward to, the time when his grandma arrives with the car and he can sit in his chair at the kitchen table, drinking Milo from a glass and talking to her while she prepares his dinner and he attends to his homework. He keeps his ears pricked, and the minute he hears the ringing voices of his neighbors, he is rushing for the door, forgetting his homework, dropping the conversation, ignoring his coat and duck boots. In the hour before dark falls, the four children sit in the gutter, leaves blowing past their ankles, Nicole's long legs folded underneath her chin. Giles potters in the mud; Joely brings her trading cards and Barbies and hoop. They chat about nothing, just childish things. They make-believe, toss gravel, peel bark off paper trees. Adrian discovers that he lives for these moments, this one gloamy hour of the day. His neighbors want him with them; on Thursday, when he's delayed helping Rory stretch canvas, Joely comes knocking like a mouse at the door, wondering what's happened to him. On Friday evening, when his first lonely school week is done, he hunkers forward round his cold white hands and, nodding up at Mr. Jeremio's house, says confidently, "You're going to live here forever, aren't you?"

Nicole is scraping a stick along the gutter and doesn't look at him. "This isn't our first house," she says. "We've had a lot of others. Dad's work sends him all over the place, and that's when we move. If they send him somewhere different from here, then we'll have to leave."

Adrian feels as if he's turning to jelly. "Do you think he will get sent away?"

Nicole shrugs, prodding leaves with the stick. "I don't know. He said Mum's too sick, now, to keep moving everywhere."

Adrian dips his head. He feels the sadness coming off Joely for a mother who can't walk or feed herself, who's visited each day by a nurse. And although he feels awful, he cannot help it: he cannot help hoping that the lady will never get well.

Nine

That evening there's a rare, rather insidious hole in Marta's hectic social life and, unable to fill the gap with her own company, she decides, at the last minute, to dine with her mother and brother. When Adrian comes indoors, he is surprised to find his gran in the flurry of fretful organization that only a visit from her daughter can incite. She dumps Adrian's dinner in front of him and hurries off to set the dining table without bothering to pronounce her customary warning about catching flu from sitting in drains.

He blows on the French fries and the single flat chop, the steam of boiled carrots churning at his throat. His chilled ears burn with the warmth of the room. His grandmother slams the oven door, polishes a tray of glasses.

"Hurry hurry hurry," she singsongs. "There's a scrap of yesterday's apple pie for your dessert, Adrian." While he dawdles over his meal, she whips up a frantic batch of lemon delicious, in her cruel haste forgetting that he reserves the right to lick the bowl.

Aunt Marta arrives in her perky blue car, bringing with her a brilliantly patterned tank top that she insists Adrian put on. "I bought it for my favorite nephew," she smiles. "You'll be adorable."

Adrian looks down at his paisleyed self in dismay. Rory, stalking down the hall, catches sight of him and stops dead. He lets his eyes grow round and wide; he rolls them dementedly in his head. Adrian starts to giggle, and Marta wheels, bristling. "Tell me what you know about fashion, Rory? Tell me!"

"He looks like a clown!"

Adrian's glad when the adults are finally cloistered in the dining room, leaving the run of the house to him. He struggles from the grip of the tank top and changes into his pajamas. He lies on the floor in front of the telly, his socked feet on the bars of the radiator. The weekend flows ahead of him like a deep and lazy river. The past few days have chewed a great chunk from him, like the bite of a shark—he feels exhausted from the sheer effort

154

of living through those massive unfriendly hours. But the weekend is here now, come to his rescue: he wishes he could slow it down, that it would stay Friday night for years, until he was older and brave.

He waits patiently in the den until he hears his grandmother bring out the empty dinner plates and take the lemon delicious from the oven. He hears her scoop the pudding into bowls and spoon onto the top of each a blot of cream and ice cream. He sits steady, watching the television but no longer seeing it, as she carries the bowls to the dining room and the door swings shut behind her. He allows a few more minutes for them to be absorbed in their talk and dessert. Then, a scavenger in search of leftovers, he scuttles to the kitchen.

The pudding tin stands in the sink. There's three or four teaspoons' worth of yellow goo stuck to the sides. He scrapes this out and shakes it onto a plate, wary of making a noise. He hears his aunt laughing, the clink of silverware on crockery. He pads to the freezer and slides out the ice-cream bucket. A platter of ice is frozen to its frigid plastic lid.

Words come suddenly through the wall. "Like a dog," Aunt Marta is saying. "Wouldn't you, if you got one?"

Adrian goes completely still, the quarry work of the

spoon halting in midgouge. His mind, fast as lightning, fills in the blanks of their conversation. They are going to get him a dog.

A dog! He's always longed for one. He would love to have a dog, somebody of his own, someone who would share his life, who wanted to be with him. A dog who'd sleep at night in his room, though Gran wouldn't let it on the bed; a dog to romp with in the garden, to gallop alongside in the park. It wouldn't matter if he spent his school days alone: he would have a dog to come home to, someone waiting and watching for him.

Standing in the kitchen, Adrian sees it all clearly: going to the pound, picking out the dog, kneeling before the dog's brown face, the dog sniffing, then licking, his hand. Bringing her home in the back seat of the car, giving her a name. Adrian's heart beats hard and fast, he wraps his arms around himself.

His aunt is talking, and he creeps closer to the door. He hears her say, "He's growing up, don't forget. He's probably getting hormonal."

"He's *nine*," Rory scoffs. "How hormonal can he be?"

Gran says, "I don't think it's him getting older; I think it's me. My mothering days are done."

"Oh, Mum!"

"I tell you, it wears me out. I haven't got the energy I used to have. It was so nice the other day, when he went to stay at Clinton's. I had a whole afternoon to myself, not worrying about a thing."

"But why does he worry you at all?" questions Rory. "He's only a little boy—"

"Yes, but he rules my days. I can't go anywhere; I can't forget myself—I've got to be here every three-thirty, collecting him from school. I get a holiday only when he does. I've got to cook a decent meal for him each night, so he doesn't waste away. He needs cleaning, clothing, carting here and there. It's hard work, rearing a child. It's not work for the old."

"You're not old, Mum," soothes Marta. "Don't be ridiculous."

Beattie smiles tightly but will not be pushed off-course. "Sometimes I think I'm bad for him. I don't have the patience I used to have. I remember when you three were young, I was much more tolerant with you. Poor Adrian's always in trouble, and that isn't good for him."

There's silence over the dinner table while her children look for inspiration in their bowls. Marta says blandly, "We've spoken about this before. I should think the person all this worrying isn't good for is you, Mum."

157

But Beattie isn't listening—her eyes have glazed; she turns her spoon. In a muted distant voice she says, "I was thinking, the other night, about those missing children. Two girls and a smaller boy—like Sookie and Maggie and Rory. I thought that if I'd lost the three of you that way—that would certainly have killed me. I would have fallen down and died. But you don't die for other people's children—only for your own. I love him, of course—I'll protect him and keep him and do whatever needs doing to get him grown; I wouldn't let him be hurt or lost; he's a part of me—but I know he isn't mine. And I sometimes worry that's the way I treat him, as if he isn't mine. I think, How can he possibly thrive?"

Her children stare across the table at her, and for some moments neither can fathom what to say. Then Marta splutters, "You should have *made* her take responsibility, Mum. What right has she got to do this to you?"

Rory groans. "*Forget* Sookie, Marta. Just forgive her, and forget."

"That's easy to say, and nice for Sookie, to leave everyone else with her mess!" Marta twists toward her mother, flames springing in her eyes. "Maybe you *should* think of doing something, if that's the way you feel,

Mum. Maybe it's best for him, and best for you. After all, he can't be happy—"

"He *is* happy! He's perfectly happy!"

Marta disregards her brother. "I'm not saying you *must,* Mum. But it's like I was saying: if you bought a dog and realized the breed didn't suit you—that it needed more exercise than you could give it, or ate more than you could afford—then it would be right, wouldn't it, to put it somewhere it got proper attention? That would be a kindness to the animal itself, wouldn't it?"

"You disgust me," Rory sighs. "I wish you wouldn't speak any more."

"At least I'm *trying*! I want to do what's best for Mum! Hasn't she got any rights?"

Beattie listens without interest as they sink their verbal fangs into one another, their lifelong rivalry taking no prisoners, sacrificing innocents, as real as a stench in the room. She feels, as she sits there, a sudden toothy hatred for her children, and wonders what error she and Lester made, to produce three such graceless offspring. Adrian, she thinks, is the only worthwhile thing ever to come from them. She clatters two bowls together, fracturing the quarrel's momentum. "I know what you're saying,

Marta," she says, "and I'm grateful you're concerned. But I'll keep him—he needs a family; he needs a home. He can be the comfort of my old age. And at least he's not always bickering, like some children I could name."

She hoists herself to her feet and collects the crockery while they watch, amused and impressed and pleased, more than anything, that this well-worn conversation topic has been dealt with successfully once again. They know nothing will come of it—it's left no mark on their minds; they can rehash it afresh next week and pretend, as always, that they've made headway on a vital matter, that they have not simply been wading through mud. By the time she returns with the coffee, they'll be happily ripping up something new.

She pushes past the swinging door, the bowls rocking on a palm. The kitchen is empty and tinged with coolness; from the den wafts the sound of the TV. She reminds herself that they must keep their voices down, given some of these walls have ears.

Adrian should know better than to eavesdrop. Not a year has passed since he stood listening in the hallway of this very house, just out of sight of the kitchen. Subsiding at his knees that day had been a garbage bag packed with all he owned. He'd been instructed to take the bag to the spare room, but he had hesitated on rounding the kitchen doorway and flattened himself to the wood-paneled wall. He can still remember how warm and smooth the wood had felt between his shoulder blades.

In the kitchen, Adrian's father was talking to Beattie. "I need to be free," the man had pleaded. "This isn't the life for me."

Beattie swears later that she'd craved to slap his face. "Lester's not cold in his grave," she said. "This isn't quite the time."

"Lester loved Adrian. He would be happy to know his grandson was here. It'll be company for you—for him and for you."

"Don't you say Lester's name." Beattie was murderous. "I won't hear it from you."

The rubber soles of the father's boots squelched across the linoleum; Adrian had turned his eyes away, as if doing so would hide him. He caught sight of his reflection in the hallway mirror, an undersized fair-haired boy wearing a trim navy coat. Inside the coat's collar was stitched a tag on which his mother had printed his name. He heard a match struck, the crackle of a cigarette. There'd been a long pause where nothing was said, but

Beattie was the only one thinking. Adrian's father had already decided what he was going to say.

"How can you do this?" the woman asked eventually. "He's your son."

"Well, so Sookie says." The man tried to sound casual, bohemian enough not to care. "She's not exactly reliable."

Beattie gagged. "Don't you dare! Don't you *dare*! You're not a father's boot lace, you!"

The smell of smoke found the boy in the hall. There was squelching as the man recrossed the room, crackling as he burned his cigarette. "Look," he said, "that's by the by. We have to do what's best for him. I can't take care of him, and that's all there is to it. I need to be free."

"Free." Beattie growled out the word. "You scoundrel. If Lester were here—"

"If Lester was here I know what he'd say, and so do you." A cheerful jankling marked the plucking up of keys. "He's no trouble, you know. Amuses himself, doesn't say much. He's tame—he's *boring*. You'll hardly notice he's here."

Beattie had followed the man to the door, waving her fists, assuring him in a demon hiss that, in doing this, he had forsaken all his rights. The man had pushed the screen door so forcefully that it hit the side of the house.

162

Adrian had hefted the garbage bag and walked down the hall to the spare room—*his* room—where he sat on the bed listening to his father's car burl away. In those minutes he had found it difficult to breathe. He slipped from his coat and hung it in the closet, the hangers knocking metallically. The downy skin of his bare arms was unmarked, but it shouldn't have been that way: the word *boring* felt branded into him with the blistering burn of an iron. His father thought him boring, a thing to be rid of. *There is nothing good about me.*

Now, Adrian sits on the same bed, staring down at the same arm. The blind over his window isn't down, and the darkness beyond the glass looks like space he could step into and run through. He should never have gone near the kitchen, should never have let himself hear the few words that he had. Still, better he did—better to know. It's his bedtime, but he suffers from a tiredness that feels beyond the reach of sleep. He has spent what seems like his entire life being driven from person to person and place to place. Like the bundle that gets handed about in the game of pass the parcel, he's been unwrapped and made smaller as he's been pushed from each to the next. He is haunted by the prospect of losing the last thin layer that protects him—he doesn't want to know what he'll

163

look like then, can't bear to think how he'll feel. But he knows where he will be, when that final thing happens. He'll be at a place like St. Jonah's, a *special* place, a place built to take care of children such as he.

Rory is surprised when the boy taps on his door. It is late, nearly midnight, and he is propped against his pillows sketching landscapes to calm himself. Marta's visits always fill her brother with such turbulence that it takes him hours to fall asleep, but Adrian's room had been darkened and peaceful when Rory glanced inside it on his way to the bathroom. The boy is apparently wide awake now. He stands in the doorway holding the sea monster painting in his arms. "I don't want this," he says, and lowers the canvas to the floor.

Rory's a little taken aback. "What's the matter? Don't you like it?"

"There's no sea monsters," the child replies dully. "It's stupid to pretend."

His uncle considers him; he tucks the pencil behind an ear and lays the sketchbook aside. He leans forward, so his elbows touch his knees. He says, "You know what that thing was, Adrian—that dead thing they dragged out of the sea? It was just a fish—just a big dead basking shark. You're right—there's no sea monsters. But that doesn't matter. It's not stupid to pretend."

"Yes it is." The boy doesn't move, standing with vast stillness in his racing-car pajamas, hands hanging loose by his sides. The lamplight has bleached his face and bare feet; behind him, the blackness of the hallway hulks like something grimly alive. "You should never tell lies."

A frown slices the flesh between Rory's eyebrows. "Pretending isn't lying, Adrian. You know the difference between pretending and lying, don't you?"

"Yes," the boy answers, "I do. But I don't think you do."

Rory hesitates. Night air finds its way down his spine. "What do you mean?"

"I mean *you* tell lies." Adrian's voice is mossy, bedraggled. "You told me I wouldn't have to go away. You promised. I *promise*, you said."

"But you're not—you're not going anywhere—"

Anger pinches the child's face. "Stop telling lies," he says stonily. "I'm not listening to you anymore."

Rory feels a twitch of the temper that's chewed his ankles ever since the night he crashed the car, a temper that skulks like an eel in a cave, that darts out with puncturing teeth. He waves a hand, blotting out the boy. "Believe whatever you like, then. See if I care."

Adrian sets his mouth. He wants to hurt Rory as much as Rory has hurt him. He dredges up the worst insult he knows. "You're crazy," he whispers. "You're scared to go outside. There's only birds and grass out there. You're a crazy loon."

"Get to bed, Adrian," his uncle says icily, "before I tan your hide."

For a moment Adrian does not budge, determined to seem unafraid; then he ducks back into the blackness, which takes him whole. Rory hears him shuffling down the hall, his fingers ticking blindly along the wood paneling, the soles of his naked feet tacking, with each step, to the polish of the floor.

He sits in the garden, making plans. He won't go to St. Jonah's. That's a place for children who have no one to care for them. But Adrian has someone; he's not completely alone. He doesn't know how to find her, or where exactly she is now: hence the making of plans.

Rory has been giving him hostile looks all day. It's easier to think outside, away from him. His grandmother told him to wear his parka if he was going into the yard.

He curls his hands up inside the pockets, commanding himself to be brave.

The wind is blustering today; this morning it had rained. It's brisk, the sky is marbled, the grass is clumped and soaking. It's a day best avoided, endured indoors. Adrian's ears smart with the buffeting, the tip of his nose is numb. But it's better to be outside, watchful, here on the slope of the lawn: from here he can see anyone approaching—there's no fence in front of him; there's somewhere for him to run. In the junction of the empty streets, he feels the liberty of being alone; he could be on a mountain, or the moon.

His knees are black from pressing into the grass. He wonders what kind of creature he is, what it is about him that makes him so difficult to like, so undesirable to have around. He shunts such thoughts away.

He thinks about the dog he had, the brown dog from the pound, and a part of him mourns for a thing that never was.

Tomorrow, then.

He hears the swing of his neighbor's front door and looks up to see Nicole. She must have spotted him at the base of the tree because she strides with her usual authority across the road, over the lawn, right up to where he hunches, as if her dominion extends everywhere. She stands glaring down at him, hands clamped on her hips. "What are you doing?"

"Nothing."

"Well, you look dumb." She drops like a puppet to her knees, clawing her fingers in the grass. The sleeves of her sweater become dusted with rain. She stretches her arms, supple as a cat, smiling steelishly at him. "Guess what?"

"What?"

"I know where they are."

He has looked askance to a garden bed, embarrassed and apprehensive with her proximity; now his head snaps around, his gray eyes thin. "Who?"

"You know."

He doesn't believe her—he wishes that for once she would tell the truth—but it's as if his skin is convinced, as if his mouth believes her. "How did you find them?"

"That's my secret. We know what each other thinks."

A line of whiteness glints at her lips; Adrian folds himself up warily. "Where are they?"

She leans against the tree trunk, her sweater jeweled by rain. "What will you give me for showing you?"

". . . What do you want?"

"The Slinky?"

Adrian blanches, drops his gaze to the grass. "Someone wrecked it. I threw it away."

She thinks about this. "I wouldn't have wrecked it, if you'd given it to me."

He nods but says nothing, plucking a weed and rolling it to pulp between his fingers. Nicole sits on her heels, chewing the flesh of her cheek. It seems they are at stalemate, their conversation possibly over. The wind lashes the crisp leaves on the ambar, chases the fallen ones across the lawn. The weather makes the girl's nose run, and she sniffs brutally. A moment passes; she shuffles forward on her knees. She says, "I know what you can give me. Give me your regret for not giving the Slinky to me."

He doesn't understand, addled by her looming teeth and eyes. She punches the earth impatiently, squeals, "Say it!"

"Say what?"

"Say you regret it!"

"I regret it," he intones.

Satisfied, she settles back. "Meet me this evening, before it gets too dark. You'll be frightened, but you can't be a coward. You must be prepared for whatever happens—prepared for *everything*. You'll never be the same again."

169

Though he doubts all she says, there's a quaver of fear. "Where will I meet you?"

"In the park—where we buried the bird. That's the secret place, Adrian. The place that will give us strength. The strength of the bird."

He remembers how fragile the bird had felt in his hands, a powder puff of nothing but feather and air. "Bring a flashlight," Nicole's saying, "and a knife, if you can. A cloth also, to shield your eyes."

He nods deeply. "All right."

"This evening, before the sky gets dark."

She makes some signals around him with her fingers, casting an elaborate spell. Then she leaps to her feet and bounds away, anteloping through the grass. She runs across the road and into her house, slamming the door behind her. The sound of it booms along the deserted street. Adrian returns his hands to his pockets and lays his plans anew.

Ten

When he goes inside, his grandmother instantly detects his grubby knees. She rains down on him threats of a horrible death, all this suffering the invariable result of sitting on waterlogged lawn. "I'm sorry, Gran," he says, and his weary contrition is enough to silence, for a second, the torrent of noise boiling from her. Her face wrestles with a gamut of emotions. When she bends down, Adrian skips away nervously. She grips his wrist and pulls him close and whisks, with brisk precision, a clover from his hair.

"Off you go," she says. "Go and get changed. I don't want you getting sick."

He tramps to his room, trousers clammy at the knees. In the privacy of his bedroom, he changes his clothes. He searches his dresser for the warmest sweater, the thickest jeans, the longest socks, the strongest boots. When he puts them all on, he feels swaddled and hot.

He tips his school bag upside down: out of it drops a lead pencil, a ball of rainbowed sandwich paper, and the wrapper of a long-gone Wagon Wheel. He stuffs into the emptied satchel a scarf and a miniature flashlight, which is really just a key chain. He adds a pair of socks and some underwear, slipping these into an inner compartment that Nicole, should she raid the bag, will hopefully overlook.

He sits gripping his ankles, thinking. He doesn't know what else to bring. He has no practice in running away. Until now he's always stayed where he was put. Even now, he's not truly running away. He's going *to* something, as much as away from something else. His mother, when he finds her, will never let him become a child of St. Jonah's.

When he finds her. The words are like a stagger, something important gone bung. He has qualms innumerable about embarking on a search for his mother when he has no idea how to begin, no knowledge of where she is or how to go about finding her. He thinks about sleeping out in the night, how cold and unpleasant that will be.

The satchel is not spacious enough to hold a blanket, but another sweater fits in when he rams it down hard.

What he'll do is ask for help. She always told him, when he was just a little kid walking to and from school alone, *If you're frightened, ask for help*. He had never needed to do so, and now as he takes the advice out and readies himself to brandish it, he sees how keen and glossy and decisive it is, a weapon more effective for never having been used.

One thing is certain: if he stays here, he is doomed. Under the ambar he'd decided to leave tonight: tomorrow is a place that can no longer be relied upon, and once he's in the park with Nicole, he'll already be halfway gone anyway. There is, in addition, the faint possibility that Nicole truly does know where the children are. If he were to help find them, he doesn't think his grandmother would send him away. She would probably look differently on a boy who did something so heroic. His doubts and loneliness would become just memories, signposts that pointed the way to being brave.

He buckles the satchel and sits down on his bed.

While Beattie is making Rory turn the mattress of the big bed, he rushes on socked feet to the kitchen and rummages through the cracker tin. There's not much in there—spongy Saladas, broken shards—but he scoops out a salty handful and pushes them up his sleeve. He returns the tin to its shelf and sweeps the crumbs from the bench. Crackers prickle the soft skin of his arm. He slips open the drawer where his grandmother keeps the knives.

In the hall, something catches his eye. He slides to a halt and traces his step. The cherub bowl squats on the mantelshelf; the cherub is looking at him. The cherub customarily faced Royal Doulton and continued to do so after she was gone; now it's turned and smiling at him. Adrian steps tentatively past the doors of the living room, his heart pulsing at his ribs. He approaches the mantel on the balls of his feet. To the cherub he whispers, "What do you want?"

Its apple-plump face is raised to him, the eyes curved over bulbous cheeks. Its hands on its thighs look lively, starfish of wicked intent. Adrian extends a finger, touching it to the small of the cherub's back. "You can't come with me," he says.

Why not?

I'll get in trouble.

You're in trouble anyway.

Adrian hesitates. The cherub smiles sunnily. *It wasn't asking much, was it, what you asked from them.*

He hears Beattie directing the making of the bed, Rory's intolerant sighs. They will be occupied just a minute more. The bowl has always been a comfort to him, and might be so again.

I will be a comfort, Adrian. When you're alone.

He hasn't the space, not in his slight satchel. *But there's nothing to a cherub, not without his bowl.*

Adrian lifts the cherub by its head; the lid, soldered to the *putto*'s calves, rises off the bowl. There's a tidy weight to the lid and cherub; it's glacial and awkward as an ice pick when he tucks it against his skin. The bowl stands on the shelf, pert on shapely legs. Like a vault that's been opened, it gives off the smell of bronze. Adrian steps away, considering, and decides that, although the bowl gapes like a wound, the absence of its lid and cherub should go unnoticed for at least a while.

Jammed into his satchel are the sweater, the socks, the underpants, the scarf, the flashlight, the cherub, the crackers, the knife. These few items make the bag so global and solid, it's like a medicine ball perched on his back. Adrian slips the satchel off and prods it, but it holds its swollen form. None of the goods can be abandoned—they're each in their own way vital to him—so he resolves to live with the difficulty. He hefts the bag and slips his arms through the strap, settling the leather at the nape of his neck. His hands are free, his shoulders bearing the load; the bulging satchel looks like some terrible growth on his spine, the kind of hump that bent people double hundreds of years ago.

He's just a child, and he knows that: he knows his plan is futile, that all of this will come to nothing, that he has absolutely no chance of finding his mother. He knows he'll be sleeping in his bed tonight, rather than under a shrubbery. But if he blocks out that knowledge, if he prepares to succeed and tries to *believe,* something miraculous may occur—others have succeeded before him, and maybe so will he. One thing is certain: nothing miraculous will happen if he stays.

When the sky clouds over, he stands up. His Batman clock says it's five. He's become stiff and cold sitting on his bed, and his legs tingle with the fresh flow of blood. The burden of the satchel tips him toward the wall. He blows air on his hands to warm them and has another idea: he paws through the dresser until he unearths a pair of knitted mittens. Pleased, he puts them in a pocket, but feels, too, a vague qualm: he wonders what other simple yet blessed item he is forgetting to bring.

The sky is powdered livid; these winter evenings grow rapidly dark, and Adrian is glad he must hurry. He would like to say goodbye to his uncle and gran but worries that, if he does so, he will never leave. They won't let him, or he'll decide not to go. So he waits until the coast is clear, when Beattie's unpegging washing from the line and Rory's settled down with coffee and cigarettes, then yells from the hallway, "I'm going out to play. OK? I'm going across the street." Nothing answers, but he knows that his uncle, in the den, will have heard. Without lingering any longer, he slips past the front door.

Adrian runs down the road, the satchel thumping on his spine, the raw air scouring his lungs. The street is damp and vacant, and he is the only thing that moves, the sole survivor of an unexpected ice age. His feet fly along the footpath, the cords of the parka flicking his thighs. The satchel tries relentlessly to slow his pace, to turn him around. He clenches his fists and powers on.

When he reaches the park, he runs between trees to the track, which is puddled with shallow rain pools. The stones make a crunching sound as they're tamped below his boots. His nose and fingers throb with cold as he runs; his cheeks are warmly flushed. In the grassy center of the park, a pair of white ibis step on legs as long as his own. Their disregard of him is complete, but other birds see him coming and flap sluggishly away. He leans into the bend of the track, the trees flashing by, the sky like a slab of mother-of-pearl, a gravestone polished with pink. The sky is a shell enclosing the park, a brittle roof over the land: sound ricochets off the grayness, pings curtly, goes nowhere.

He remembers where they buried the bird among tangles of eucalypt root, and as he nears the place he slows, breath steaming out of him. He can see the tree but not Nicole, and as he walks he spins a circle, scanning fretfully for her. A quick shrill whistle makes him look up and there she is, a lemur on a bough. She's wearing a purple poncho that brushes at her knees. "Did you come alone?" she asks, in a voice that's deep and dangerous.

He nods vigorously. "Yes."

"Did you tell anyone you were coming here?"

"No."

Her face is set; just her gaze moves to the bag. "Did you bring what I told you?"

He nods again, squeezing his hands.

"The knife too?"

"Uh-huh."

With this she clambers from the eucalypt, landing inelegantly before him. Leaves spin down around them. "Are you afraid?"

He shakes his head, but she seems unconvinced. "If you *are*," she warns, "you better leave now. You better not cry like a baby."

"I'm not afraid," he assures her, although he suspects he is. He wants to tell her he has run away from home, but he worries she'll laugh at him. He knows there is something ridiculous about the notion of running away. "Kneel down," she orders, and he promptly does so; the earth is slimy beneath his knees. Nicole kneels beside him and puts her hand on the grave. The soil shows no sign of having been disturbed, but the weeds Nicole had cast about are withered and bleached, contorted as bones. "Repeat after me," she tells him: *"O bird, give me strength."*

"O bird, give me strength."

"Let me fly."

"Let me fly."

"Let me see things that are hidden from other eyes."

"Let me see things hidden from other eyes."

His own eyes are shut tight, in imitation of hers. He sees, in his blindness, a ghost of the tree, a ghost of the grave. The earth is clammy, the skin of a fish. His eyes flutter open when he feels Nicole stand up. The poncho makes her lean and limbless, an obelisk. Her face is waxen and bears no expression, the face of a child saint. She turns this emptiness on him. "If we find them," she says flatly, "everyone will pay attention to us."

Adrian gets to his feet, the satchel tipping him like a toy. He has the sudden realization that she is friendless, as he is, that her days are one long exercise in whittling time. But then he thinks this cannot be, that he must be very wrong. "Come on," she says, nudging him into motion. "We must begin."

He walks alongside her, dusting weeds from his hands, the satchel slouched on his rump. Except for the gravel gritting underneath their shoes, the park is utterly quiet; already the sky has grown noticeably more dim. There are fewer birds pecking amid the shaved grass, and a haze of midges is gathering for the night. He glances at his companion, who walks like an undertaker, head down, evenly, her hands behind her back. "Where's Joely?" he asks, and his voice is as disturbing as nails on a blackboard against the silence of the field.

"At home. We don't need her."

He nods in agreement, though he does not agree. It would be more like a game, if Joely were here.

"Besides," adds Nicole, with a drop of poison, "she would be scared."

They've reached the most distant point of the track—if they continue to follow it, the path will curve and wend them back in the direction of home. Without hesitation Nicole steps off the gravel, into the surrounding trees. They're following the route they took the day they first met, weaving past the same trunks, toiling up the same hill, and now, as then, she is leading, born to command. Tall weeds and dropped twigs litter the urban forest and swipe at Adrian's shins; foggy air lurks beneath the umbrella of canopy, shiftless and stale. A bird in the branches caws threateningly, and the children shamble sideways, fearing an attack. "Come on," Nicole urges, "there's not much time!"

She storms up the hill and Adrian scrambles after her, hampered by his bulky clothes and the ballast of the satchel and by the slippery, rutted incline. They grab saplings to stop themselves sliding backward; Nicole's tasseled poncho flaps behind her like a heroine's cape. He lurches and slithers, his legs protesting, his hands scratched by trees—then the forest's abruptly finished, the hill subsiding suddenly flat, and before them, beneath a gelid sky and behind the silver wirework of fence, spreads the garish green and blueness of the local swimming pools. Nicole, breathing hard, hooks her fingers through the wire. Her sooty eyes flit from pool to pool, across the lawns, past the kiosk and swings. "She's near water," Adrian hears her whisper. "There's water."

He presses his face to the fence, feeling the steel gouge his cheekbones. Uneasily, he thinks she could be correct—there's no reason for them not to be here, in this wintry, closed-down place. "What are we going to do?" he asks.

"Go in. Find them."

He squints dubiously. There's a char-headed ibis prowling the path leading to the kiosk, but otherwise the complex is deserted. It will stay that way until summer, when the grass will brown off and the loudspeaker will crackle and laughter and splashing will carry through the forest and over the park, right into Beattie's backyard. "The gates are locked," he points out, somewhat gladly. "We can't get in."

"Yes we can. Climb the fence."

He gazes up, and up. There's a string of sagging barbed wire threaded along the top of the fence. The wall of cyclone fencing shimmers and wavers, pretending to be frail. It can be climbed—Rory has told him how, as a teenager, he and his friends often climbed this fence on balmy nights, to swim like seals in black solitude. Adrian can't imagine his uncle doing such things—his uncle's fingers in wire, his uncle's feet in the grass. "What if we get in trouble?"

"We won't," Nicole answers firmly. "Who would get mad, if we find them?"

Adrian swallows. He peers again at the lawn, the seeping shadows. From this distance he can see the doorways of the locker room and restrooms, but he can't tell if the doors are bolted or padlocked. Anything might be in those buildings (*anyone*). He has only an imperfect feeling for passed time, but he knows the Metfords have been missing for weeks—long enough for them to be changed, to lose their childlikeness, to become something *other*. He imagines the Thin Man leering over them like an owl; he sees shapeless piles of clothing and fallen bone. The more Adrian stares at this windblown stretch of ground, this lonely, out-of-season place, its pools like cavities, its buildings like caves, the more clearly he understands that the children cannot be anywhere but here. This is the place they always were, there was no other place they could go, and he is filled with a freezing dread. "Maybe we shouldn't," he suggests. "Maybe we should tell someone . . ."

Nicole shies from him, disgusted. "You're frightened!"

"But—what if the man is there?"

"He *won't* be." She's scorning. "I thought you were my *friend,* Adrian."

"I am, but—"

She prods him in the shoulder. "If you don't come with me," she hisses, "I'll hate you forever. I'll never speak to you again."

He ogles her in panic, his fingers aching on the wire: his blood feels as though it's changed to oil when she pulls away and starts to climb. The fence rattles and shudders as she claws her way up, rippling like a tune. She will climb to the top and then into the clouds, and he jigs about in dismay. He can't, *he can't* get left behind. He can't go home without her; he cannot lose somebody else. He's not shocked to discover he's abandoned his plan, that he's no longer even pretending to be running away— he always knew he wasn't that boy, who could take his life in his hands. But he cannot, *he simply cannot*, go to sleep tonight knowing Nicole has spurned him, that he's now completely alone. "Wait!" he yelps. "Wait for me!"

He forces the rounded toe of his boot into a diamond-shaped gap in the wire and hauls himself clumsily off the ground. The satchel pulls on his shoulders, a chunky kernel of gravity, but he can't throw it off—he'll need the knife and the scarf and possibly the cherub. Nicole climbs like a monkey, her long hair swinging at her elbows, her narrow feet finding the gaps. She is nearing the top and halts only briefly to ponder the barbed wire. Adrian knows it won't dare hinder her and it doesn't—she snakes past it—and although the poncho catches in half a dozen places, she unhooks and unsnags as if this difficulty is all part of the fun. By the time Adrian reaches the peak and works his careful way over it, Nicole is close to the ground. At the height of the fence, the wind is strong and the wire wobbles and sings: Adrian clings to it with hurting hands, thinking that, were he brave enough to look around, he might see his grandmother's house. He picks his way down the reverse of the fence and drops to earth exhausted. He straightens his coat and adjusts the satchel, noting that the sky is very somber now—within the forest there are pockets of absolute pitch, and even the fence fades into the distance, camouflaged in the gloom. He rubs his crooked fingers, wishing he could put his mittens on, knowing that, if he did so, Nicole would laugh at him. He slumps beside her, miserable, while she stands on her tiptoes to examine the complex. The two smaller pools, drained of water, look condemned and desolate. The kiddies' pool has rotting leaves in the corners, a river of rain in its gully. The square pool, Adrian's favorite, has what seems to be a tree sprouting from its tiled floor, a muscular branch with leaves and twigs that's too big to have blown here on the wind. The branch's leaves are wilted but green: something living has carried this branch and propped it here, and not very long ago. This strange but definite sign of life, standing like a signal, full of secretive meaning, crimps Adrian's forehead with worry. He is afraid—of quicksand, of tidal waves, of burning, of night; he fears monsters, closets, being forgotten, going astray—and now he's fearful of a branch. "I think we should go," he says.

Nicole answers, "They are near water."

Except for the rain-river in the kids' pool, there's only one place of water. The adult pool spans the horizon, impossibly long and wide. Adrian knows it is deep at both ends, even the end that's supposedly shallow. His waggling feet have never scraped the aqua tiles that shine up from the depths. This is the serious pool, where laps are swum and races are run and athletes dive from numbered blocks — all these being things he cannot do, and he supposes, in a way, he's also scared of the pool. This evening it appears massively benign, restful and sweet smelling as a pond, making no movement beneath its off-season cover. Scattered across its plastic coat is a drift of orange leaves. The ropes that tether the cover to the edge creak placidly against the tiles. "Come on." Nicole elbows his ribs. "There's not much time."

They weave down the hill toward the big pool, Adrian lagging behind. The pool looks peaceful, the cover lies still, but there could be a whale lurking under there, some viscous creature born from the stagnant liquid and months of solitude. He wonders what flesh looks like after it has been in water so long.

The ibis has raised its curving beak and is gazing at them. Brushing through the buffalo grass, Adrian's toes clip Nicole's heels.

The children stop on the footpath, where they can hear the water sigh. The tiles and the concrete and the smoothness of the land make this place colder than anywhere, and Adrian wraps his arms around his chest.

187

Nicole picks up a pebble and flings it across the big pool. It bounces twice with dull *twack*s on the cover before spinning to a halt. She grunts, interested. To Adrian's disconcertment, she trots over to the square pool and retrieves from its basin the wayward branch, which she drags after her to the big pool. Her progress leaves a rent in the grass, and two or three loosened leaves. Adrian watches, hair blowing in his eyes. Nicole hoists the branch above her head and, with effort, launches it at the big pool. A wave reverberates through the cover as the branch skids and rolls and the ropes around the perimeter are yanked and splashed, but the plastic holds and the branch does not sink. It stays where it stops, the leaves trembling. Nicole chuffs, delighted, clapping her hands. Without a word and before Adrian can protest, she has stepped over the brink of the pool onto the cover, onto the winter water.

She takes several slow paces, sliding her feet, her hands hovering up from her sides. The ropes strain at their moorings, lifting the plastic hem clear of the water. The girl turns a slow circle, hardly daring to breathe. "Look!" she marvels. "Look at me!"

Adrian crouches at the tiled perimeter, chewing his

nails, cautiously impressed. Nicole stands on bandy spread legs, the water rollicking gently. She concentrates on her balance, watching her feet. A thin layer of liquid has flooded the cover, puddling where she stands. Her knees knock and she lurches, the cover heaves like something waking from sleep; regaining equilibrium, she lifts her eyes to him. "Look!" she calls. "They're near water, I'm near water!"

He smiles weakly, longing for her to return to land. The tiles, blue as sapphire, give off a hum of cold. Evening is staining the sky, a watercolor of smoke and cream. When he can't resist the words any longer, he says, "Nicole, you better come back . . ."

She ignores him, as he knew she would. She quakes her way across the pool until she's separated from him by a quivering expanse. She is nearing the junction where the four giant pieces of cover meet, rope stitched along the seams like thick cotton thread. Adrian sits straighter, sees water sliding past the joins. "Nicole," he says, and she flips a careless hand. The ibis is disturbed by the sounds and the scene—a sough of air makes Adrian glance over a shoulder to see it lift heavily into the sky. A buckle on the satchel's strap taps his chin, sending a shock through his jaw. The ibis swoops past the concrete cactus, climbs high to clear the monkey bars. Its neck is sinuous, plump as a bean, its long legs trail like ribbons. It is no longer a white bird, but gray. When he turns to look again at her, Nicole has reached the center of the pool. "Nicole!" he calls.

She has her back to him, and the tassels of her poncho are dripping. "Everyone will pay attention to us," she says. When she slides her foot across the plastic, a wave of water curls from her sneaker. At the sewn-up crossroads of the cover, the plastic will be weaker, the surface tension breakable, and only the ropes will be holding her up. "Nicole!" he cries.

It makes him cross when she takes another step. Frozen and frightened, annoyance makes him momentarily warm. He thinks she knows the peril she's in, just as he thinks she knows everything: when she persists in walking on water, he thinks she is simply showing off. Crossness is the final thing he will feel for her.

She drops between the plastic seams with scarcely a splash. The rope stitching yawns, then swallows her, then comes together again. This is done calmly, as though water were sand—if anything, the cover is more motionless when she's under it than when she was above. Adrian reels back from the edge, his hands coming up to his face. The slumping satchel unbalances him and he trips, legs everywhere, an elbow striking the path. He glimpses smudged sky, dandelion near his nose. He staggers to his feet and can hardly believe she's gone, though he's alone as if she were never here.

A sound comes from him, the fractious wail of a bird. From his shoulders spread two broad pale wings. He flies across the plastic, toward the vanishing point. The water sloshes under him, swelling into waves; he feels it splash his ankles, saturating his feet. His arms flail behind him as he runs, his hair streams from his eyes. His running legs are leaden, as if they plowed through snow.

He cannot leave her: he cannot do nothing. A good boy unto the end, he can not go home without her. So he tries.

The water takes him gladly.

He has no fins or wings.

It is worse than cold.

He opens his mouth to scream, and water rushes in. The satchel is a boulder strapped across his back. Inside, he feels the cherub drown, its kick of rage and fear.

The water is darker than the darkening sky. A black

shroud presses against his face, and his teeth clamp together in wool. Nicole turns and wavers and turns again. The poncho is a sail that takes her down.

His feet, kicking, touch nothing. His hands, outstretched, touch nothing. His blunt fingernails do not find rope. The cover of the pool seals the line between water and oxygen. He butts against it, but it does not lift.

Later, the cover will wrap him like skin. He'll float in still liquid like something not yet born, like something only waiting to be born and begin.

The ibis lands, swirling gnats through the air.

Beattie answers the knock on the front door. For a second or two she fails to recognize the slim balding man who stands in the gathered darkness, and her face remains unwelcomingly severe; recollection makes her bob her head in a friendly but uncommitted way. He feels her aloofness and smiles awkwardly. "I've come to relieve you of my daughter," he says. "Nicole."

"Nicole?" She knows this is one of the girls from over the way, but has no idea which one. "I don't think she's here."

"She isn't?" The man is surprised. "She said she was coming here."

Beattie sets her mouth, switching on the porch light. In the gauzy illumination of the globe, she sees how the weather has ruffled the man's scalp so the flesh there looks scalded and raw. She calls into the house, "Rory!"

Her son appears, not immediately, in the doorway of the den, and nods across the hall to the visitor. He recognizes their neighbor without difficulty, having watched him through various windows. Beattie is curt, for this doesn't interest her. "Rory, have you seen the little girl, Nicole? She told her father she was coming here."

So Rory is the first to know it, and it's he who frowns and must say, "I thought Adrian was going to Nicole's house."

The burble of the television fills the silent gap that follows, but still it is a gap, and still it is silent. Inside it, each of them thinks of the Thin Man: they think of children who are not found.

Beattie's gaze coasts along the floor and climbs the height of her son. She turns her head painstakingly, as if she is in pain, as if she is keeping shattering pain at bay. Later she will say this was the moment when she understood what had happened, that she'd turned her head knowing exactly what she would see. What she says now is, "Rory, bring my coat."

In the days to come, there'll be talk on the radio about the world becoming an unsafe place, about the good old days being gone. There will be confusion and outrage, suspicion, accusation. There will be a terrible sense of sadness in the knowledge that a child is no longer safe at play. All this will happen in the days to follow. But as the three adults come together in the stale light below the eaves, these are not the things that are said and done. Rory and Beattie look stricken at each other, and Nicole's father spreads helpless hands. "I need her to come home," he says. "Her dinner's ready, you see."

Where we are, we can hear birds. Where we are, we can see stars. Where we are, a cat's paw claws the earth. Where we are, we hear choirs sing.

Here, as always, we hold each other's hands.

Where we are, we feel thunder. Where we are, we hear dogs howl. Here, swallows catch insects. Here, we feel church bells.

Here rain falls on our eyes.

Where we are, weeds grow pale. Dusk seals our lips, wind knots our hair. Where we are, cracks open in the dark.

Worms slap like whips.

Where we are, we have grown thin. There is water in our ears, the mud has made us gray.

Where we are, morning wipes us clean.
We hear Mother speak our names.

We are here; *here*

Where we are, winter grass is growing.
Where we are, we feel the sun.